THE SAMURAI OF SEVILLE

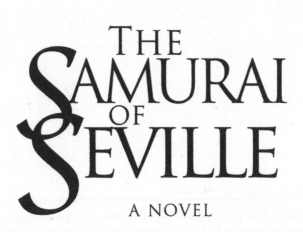

A NOVEL

JOHN J. HEALEY

Arcade Publishing · New York

First Paperback Edition 2019

Arcade Publishing books may be purchased in bulk at special discounts for sales promotion, corporate gifts, fund-raising, or educational purposes. Special editions can also be created to specifications. For details, contact the Special Sales Department, Arcade Publishing, 307 West 36th Street, 11th Floor, New York, NY 10018 or arcade@skyhorsepublishing.com.

Arcade Publishing® is a registered trademark of Skyhorse Publishing, Inc.®, a Delaware corporation.

Visit our website at www.arcadepub.com.

10 9 8 7 6 5 4 3 2 1

Library of Congress Cataloging-in-Publication Data is available on file.

Cover design by Erin Seaward-Hiatt
Cover illustration: Calderón Studio

Print ISBN: 978-1-948924-21-4
Ebook ISBN: 978-1-62872-785-2

Printed in the United States of America

For Soledad

– PART ONE –

– PART ONE –

– I –

In which an oath is given and a sword received

To those who fought for him and to those who fled his sword, the First Lord and founder of Sendai, Date Masamune, was known as *Dokuganrya*, the one-eyed dragon. In battle his armor was black, and adorning his helmet was a sliver of gold shaped like the moon's waxing crescent.

When his sister Mizuki turned sixteen, she married a wellborn warrior who fought at her brother's side. By eighteen, she was a childless widow. In her twenty-first year, she became the mistress of her brother's chief advisor Katakura Kojuro and conceived a son. When the boy was born, she asked her brother to name him, and Date Masamune called him Shiro. Like his paternal grandfather, a monk who became a Samurai, the boy was born with six fingers on his right hand. It was an omen of promise and a coveted advantage in swordsmanship.

Katakura Kojuro lived with his wife and family within the estate of the Shiroishi Castle, which had been given to him by Date Masamune. After Shiro was born, Kojuro was harried by his wife for fathering such an illustrious bastard and nagged into ending his affair with Mizuki. She raised the boy with Date Masamune and his wife and children within the walls of the far grander Sendai Castle. Mizuki was long and willowy, and Shiro grew tall and handsome with well-formed limbs.

In his thirteenth year, the boy became a Samurai, and the Lord summoned him to his private garden. Shiro had never been there before. The pebbles of the garden were raked to perfection, and there was a scent of wet pine and cedar. He found Date Masamune kneeling on dark wide floorboards so polished he could see his reflection. Off to the side there were paper panels with borders painted a deep red.

'Your mother is my only sister,' the Lord said, 'but this castle and my name must go to my sons. She is not betrothed to your father, and his castle and name shall go to the sons he has had with his lawful wife.'

Shiro tried not to stare at the scar where the Lord's left eye had been. Gouged out in battle, it had been sewn shut many years before and over time had smoothened into a marbled star.

'But the blood of my father runs through you,' the Lord continued, 'and my blood runs through you, and you have sworn fealty to me upon this day and you will follow the Way of the Warrior. Tell me you know all of this to be true.'

They were kneeling side by side facing a boulder with moss growing in the crevices. The boulder rested against a stunted *Akamatsu* tree.

'I know all of this to be true, my Lord.'

As Date Masamune next spoke, he kept his eye upon the boulder, never once looking at the boy, and when he finished, the boy knew it was time to rise and leave.

'Nevertheless you are a Prince,' he said, 'and shall be as a son to me, and wherever you go I too shall be with you, and if anyone ever scorns you it will be as if they are scorning me. For as long as you live our warrior's life, you and your descendants shall never lack for anything. Behind me is the sword that was mine in the battle of Odawara. My name and seal are etched upon it, and now it is yours.'

Masamune lowered his head. Shiro rose and bowed and took the sword and raised it to his head before backing away, holding it out in front of him. As he passed by the guards, they bowed to him, for they had heard what the Lord had said. Masamune stayed for another half an hour observing the bark of the tree and the damp place where the boulder met the earth.

– II –

In which a mistress is revealed

María Luisa Benavides Fernández de Córdoba y de la Cerda was a direct descendant of Isabel de la Cerda and Bernardo Bearne, Conde de Medinaceli. The baby girl's parents, *sevillanos* with a palace in the city and numerous estates, were of royal blood dating from the reign of Alfonso the Wise.

Ignoring strenuous protest from the family priest, María Luisa's father Don Rodrigo had the child baptized in the fetid waters of the Guadalquivir River. Her mother, Doña Inmaculada Gúzman de la Cerda, amused by her husband's eccentric gesture, began to call her daughter 'Guada.' This led to confusion when the child was twelve and lived for a time at the court of Philip the Third in Madrid. She spent much time there with her cousin Guadalupe Medina. Guadalupe, who detested the shorter 'Lupe,' insisted on being called Guada as well, thus forcing courtiers to address the young ladies by their full names. But behind their backs, María Luisa was known as Guada the Fair.

Rodrigo's son and namesake displayed a preference for other boys early on. Regular beatings and a mistress his father paid for proved useless. When the heir was admitted to the priesthood, continuance of the family line fell to Guada, for Doña Inmaculada refused to have any more children.

Shortly into her fifteenth year, Guada's engagement was announced to a distant cousin, the Duke of Denia, whose properties would increase the already considerable family holdings three-fold. She thought the boy, who was called Julian and who was two years older than she, handsome and refined. She informed her mother that her *prometido* possessed 'a poetic disposition.' Walking on garden paths under the shade of chestnut blossoms behind the San Geronimo Monastery in Madrid, strolling through the rose garden at her great aunt's finca 'La Moratalla' near Palma del Río, and sitting under shade at the beach in Sanlúcar de Barrameda observed by chaperones, the two youths allowed themselves to confuse instinct with love.

One day, she started to wonder about having children and expressed concern to her mother. 'I know what happens,' Guada said. 'I have seen dogs by the walls of the Alcázar and our own horses here in the corral, and I have seen my brother bathing, and I have examined myself carefully.'

'Then what more can I tell you child?'

They were in her mother's chamber in a family finca outside the town of Carmona. From where they sat, they could see rolling fields of new green wheat so vast that when Guada half-shut her eyes, they transformed into a verdant sea. Standing behind Doña Inmaculada was the Moorish woman from across the strait who combed her hair each morning and who hardly spoke Castellano.

'I know what happens,' Guada said again, 'but I do not know how it happens, the steps. How it comes about.'

'Under the eyes of God,' her mother said, leaning her head forward with each stroke of the wide ivory comb. 'The body knows what to do. There is nothing to learn. It may be unpleasant, as is the case with other corporal functions, but it is a natural thing.'

'Is it unpleasant?'

'Not if your husband is gentle.'

'Was father not gentle?'

'Women of our station do not enjoy it. Although a lower sort is known to.'

'You have not answered my question.'

'Your father is many things, but gentle is not one of them. I was as young as you and knew far less. Your father was nervous and, despite all his talk, inexperienced. He felt the passion of desire and I a passion for obedience.'

'And did it stay that way?'

'We've never discussed it. And since you were born, we have not shared a bed. As we know, your father finds that sort of companionship elsewhere.'

Guada left the encounter more troubled than soothed. She had hoped her mother would humor her and assuage her fears with the Andalusian wit she was known for. But instead, Inmaculada's normally cloistered northern roots had revealed themselves and bristled like Castilian steel.

Upon their return to Sevilla, Doña Inmaculada received a visit from her elderly aunt Doña Soledad Medina y Pérez Guzman de la Cerda, who brought a gift of gossip with her that put both women in a state of high agitation. On the following morning, Inmaculada sought out her husband after mass, before the midday meal, on the day before he was to travel to Madrid. He was in his study enjoying a glass of an amber toned Manzanilla sherry.

'I must speak with you about a matter most pressing,' she said, looking at him straight on.

'Pray tell,' said Don Rodrigo, only half-listening, expecting a complaint about some domestic squabble or yet another worry on his spouse's part about a new physical woe, imagined or real. The obsession she had nurtured since they had stopped having relations, speaking endlessly of illness and disease, tired him. As she spoke, he contemplated the ring on the middle finger of his right hand embellished with his coat of arms.

'What do you think of Don Julian?' Inmaculada asked, taking him by surprise.

'In what regard?'

'In every regard,' she said, surprising him further still.

'Why?'

'I'm told he has a mistress. The boy is seventeen and has a mistress twice his age who is none other than his own aunt.'

'Which aunt?' he asked her, looking away from the ring as if bidding farewell to happiness. For intuition instantly provided the answer to his question. He gazed down at the large terra-cotta floor tiles they stood upon, stained with a burnt hue that reminded him of Sicily.

'Marta Vélez,' she replied.

'That cannot be,' he said, knowing it could.

'That was my reaction exactly, but Soledad claims it is certain.'

'I sincerely doubt it.'

'Both of Marta's sons are dead. Her beastly husband stays away slaughtering game in Asturias. She is still attractive. Julian is handsome. And she is only his half-aunt from a blood point of view.

Apparently he stays with her often in Madrid and not in a separate room.'

In bed with Marta Vélez four days later, Rodrigo broached the topic.

'Where on earth did you hear such a thing?' Marta Vélez demanded, pulling her peignoir shut from his suddenly undeserving eyes.

'So you are not denying it.'

'I will not even acknowledge such foul gossip.'

'Because it is true.'

'Don't be a hapless bore.'

At court the following day, Don Rodrigo called upon his childhood friend Don Francisco Gómez de Sandoval y Rojas, the First Duke of Lerma. Rodrigo was a Grandee of Spain. The Sandovals, also from Sevilla, but nobles of lesser strata, had to work and scheme for their money. The Duke, who had insinuated himself into the life of Philip the Third when the boy was still a young prince, now ran the empire, amassing great fortune for himself and his family. But one thing he wanted and could not have despite his power and ambition was what Rodrigo had inherited by birth. They got along and used each other well. Few dared to cross Rodrigo for fear of offending the Duke of Lerma, and the Duke enjoyed tossing the name of his aristocratic friend around in a manner that made it seem like he, too, was a member of that special fold.

The Duke of Lerma's only claim to masculine appeal derived from the charisma radiated by his power. Nevertheless, he considered himself handsome and had many women more than pleased to agree. His office at the royal palace separated the halls and rooms permitted to nobles from those reserved for the King and his family. As he listened to his friend, he regarded himself in a large Venetian mirror donated to the crown by the Cardinal Bishop of Sabina, Scipione Borghese, the Pope's brother. His desk, simple but massive, had come from a looted synagogue in Toledo. Don Rodrigo stood by a window gazing down at an enclosed garden that had a fountain in the middle where a priest read from a breviary.

'She denies it,' Rodrigo said. 'But I could tell she was lying.'

'Did you tell her this bit of news before or after you had your way with her?'

'Before.'

'Which is to say you did not have your way then, did you?'

'This is serious.'

'Nonsense.'

'The boy is about to marry my daughter.'

'What would you have me do? Drag Marta Vélez before the Inquisition? What is the crime? Where is the heresy? She is well regarded by the King, ignored by her dullard husband, and she's lost her sons. She probably just dotes on the boy. You should be grateful.'

'Grateful.'

The Duke began to laugh.

'You are mocking me,' Rodrigo said, exasperated. 'Maybe she is innocent and telling the truth.'

'I certainly hope not,' the Duke replied.

'How can you say such a thing?'

'It's too delicious.'

'You, sir, are a vile man.'

'And you an angry one at the thought of being cuckolded by your mistress and future son-in-law. You must take the news with philosophy, humor even, some of that compassion you always accuse me of lacking. And surely once the boy marries he will stop seeing her, and you can have her all to yourself again.'

In which Shiro meets Yokiko and a journey is explained

At the urging of the Lord, Shiro was exposed to barbarians from an early age. He was sent to Edo to apprentice with the seaman and navigator William Adams, an Englishman who, to the great frustration of the Portuguese Jesuits, had been saved from execution by the Shogun Tokugawa Ieyasu. When Shiro worked with him, Adams was already adopting Japanese dress and manners. He taught the boy the fundamentals of astronomy, geometry, and cartography, how to sail, and he instructed the young Samurai to speak and read in English. His fellow crewmate from the shipwrecked *Liefde*, the Dutch carpenter Pieter Janszoon, taught Shiro how to work with wood and how ships were designed. The Franciscan Friar from Sevilla, Luis Sotelo, protected by Lord Date Masamune himself, taught the boy Latin, Greek, and Spanish. Exposure to the cultures and tongues of these English and Spanish tutors, the former reserved, practical, and melancholic, the latter expansive, conniving, and opportunistic, widened Shiro's world in ways that set him apart from his Samurai brethren.

The Portuguese, and then the Spanish, had attempted to bring their religion to the kingdom. Jesuits made converts in the southern shogunates. Shiro and his fellow Samurai found the foreign faith tiresome, condescending, and strangely complex. But some Japanese listened, and others far wiser, like the Shogun Tokugawa Ieyasu and Lord Date Masamune, lent, for a time, a liberal ear to their rant motivated by other interests. A powerful earthquake had devastated areas key to internal commerce, and new markets were needed. After learning about the riches of Spain and Italy, Date Masamune protected Father Sotelo, allowing him to preach in a limited manner. If the price for trading with such powerful barbarians was to allow their religious stories to sink fragile roots into his treasured soil, so be it. He reasoned it was worth the effort, to observe what might come of it. His battles had been fought. His campaigns had been successful. His castle was complete. There was little left to prove.

As Shiro grew into a young man, he reflected much upon these things. He had heard the tale of the twenty-six Christians crucified and pierced to death in 1597, some of whom were Japanese. They had been ridiculed for the stubbornness of their beliefs and driven like errant swine through the streets, taunted and stoned all the way to Nagasaki. After being tied to crosses and run through with spears, the barbarian bodies had been opened and examined. To the consternation of all who were present, it was clear their insides were the same as those of the noblest Samurai.

The Japanese word for anyone born in another land was *nanban*. But from William Adams and Father Sotelo, he learned the concept was universal. The English word barbarian and the Spanish word *bárbaro* came from the Latin *barbaria* meaning foreign country, from the Greek *barbaroi* meaning 'all that are not Greek.' So this was confusing to Shiro, for it seemed other races from other lands shared the same prejudice. Despite certain physical variations of skin tone, hair, and the shape of one's eyes, everything else appeared to be the same. The greatest differences, he realized, were questions of custom, of relative delicacy, scientific knowledge, of religion. Though the barbarian ships were better adapted for ocean travel and their muskets more fearsome, their swords were infinitely inferior, their eating habits revolting, their aversion to cleanliness a nose-holding scandal. Their religion was intrusive and bizarre.

In the spring of 1612, when Shiro was eighteen years old, after an official exhibition of swordsmanship within the grounds of the Sendai Castle, he approached the Lord and asked him for counsel regarding the treatment of foreigners. The Lord, unsmiling, asked him to elaborate and heard him out, and when Shiro had finished, he said to him, 'Come with me.'

He followed the Lord into the Arms Chamber where servants removed his battle gear, wrapping each piece in silk before placing it on varnished shelves that stood next to displays of ancient swords, spears, bows, and arrows. Upon the Lord's command, they did the same for Shiro, and he was honored by it. Then the Lord removed the clothing he wore beneath and stepped into a robe waiting for him. Shiro was told to do the same.

From there they walked through a long and narrow hall that led away from the area where the Lord lived with his wife and family. 'Your concerns please me,' he said to the young man. 'All that you have seen and thought about reflects the clarity of your intellect and confirms the validity of my judgment. My own sons, even those older than you, are still too brash, too impulsive, too shallow, too quick to boast, too quick to draw their swords.'

Shiro was honored again and expressed his gratitude.

They came to an area that Shiro had only heard about by way of rumor, a lush garden protected by tall extensions of the castle walls camouflaged by towering trees and climbing plants. The garden had a wild look to it despite the fact that every tree and shrub had been carefully chosen and planted. A small stream ran through the center. Birds in cages hung from fruit trees. Two large wooden tubs rested in the center, and then, crossing the stream by way of a small wooden bridge, the path divided into two, each one leading to a one-room bungalow located at the garden's opposite ends.

A beautiful woman he had never seen before, wearing a simple blue kimono, stood by one of the tubs that was already filled with hot water. She bowed to the Lord and then bowed to him. The Lord came up to her and turned around, allowing her to remove his robe. After being scrubbed clean, he immersed himself in the water. With his eyes, he instructed the same be done for Shiro. They soaked for almost half an hour before the Lord beckoned for the woman to approach him. He whispered something into her ear that caused her to back away and disappear. Some minutes later she returned with towels. The Lord left the tub and pointed to one of the bungalows. 'I am going there. You go to the other one. Later we shall have tea and speak about the future.' Shiro put his hands together and bowed, watching the Lord walk off. The woman followed some paces behind. He watched them enter the small house and slide the door shut behind them.

When he stepped from the tub, he felt uncomfortable for being naked and dripping wet in an outdoor garden. No towel or robe had been left for him. He wondered if guards posted on the walls could see him. He crossed the small bridge over the stream and walked upon the well-raked path leading to the bungalow assigned to him. The pebbles of the path were smooth and easy to step upon. The air smelled of apple and plum blossoms. He wondered who fed the birds.

He let himself into the bungalow. Its floor was made from boards of polished cedar. A bed was unfurled perpendicular to the entrance. There was no decoration of any sort, but the shapes of the plants and branches outside could be seen as shadows against the paper walls. A small stove steamed over a fire in a pit at the center of the floor. A young girl, no more than sixteen, knelt by the stove, awaiting his arrival, holding a towel and a robe. When he made to cover himself, she turned her head away. Then she stood and approached him and, saying nothing, began to carefully dry him with the towel.

Two hours later, he met the Lord in a tearoom apart from the garden. In this room birds flew freely and perched on the rafters. The monk preparing the tea was old and blind and had served Date Masamune's father faithfully. The Lord raised his cup toward Shiro.

'I hear it went well.'

Shiro bowed his head.

'Your modesty becomes you,' the Lord continued. 'You may spend the night here with her and return to your barrack in the morning.'

Shiro blushed.

'Your concern with barbarians pleases me, for you are to set forth upon a great journey—as my eye and ears. You may have heard how a nobleman in my province called Hasekura Tsunenari has been condemned for corruption and shall be beheaded. I have known him since my early youth and am saddened. He fought with me in many campaigns. In deference to his family's honor, I have pardoned his son, Hasekura Tsunenaga, from the same fate. The son is twice your age and will lead a delegation for me across the great seas along with twenty-one Samurai including ten from the Shogun and twelve of mine. They will accompany one hundred and twenty merchants, sailors, servants, and assorted barbarians, the most important of which will be the Spaniards Father Sotelo and the seaman Sebastian Vizcaino. Tokugawa Ieyasu and Tokugawa Hidetada have commended this mission to me. The ship is being built by the Shogun's Admiral, Mukai Shogen Tadakatsu, who constructed a number of frigates with your friend William Adams. The vessel will be ready to sail this autumn.'

Here he paused, took another sip of the tea, and then pointed at Shiro directly. 'You shall not speak of this meeting of ours to anyone, not even to Hasekura Tsunenaga. You shall comport yourself like the rest of your warrior colleagues, but with your senses open, for I will need to know upon your return that the truth is being spoken to me. Do you understand?'

'Yes my Lord. For how long shall I be away?'

'Two years at least.'

That night after the girl, Yokiko, had bathed and fallen asleep beside him, he lay awake and wondered about her. She was the daughter of a prisoner and had been taken as booty and trained to serve the Lord by his mistress. She had been with Date Masamune once and with his sons and was treated well otherwise. She felt she was fortunate because her beauty had spared her from a harsher fate. As she told him these things, he tried to make sense of his emotions. Neither of them mentioned what might occur when she grew older.

Looking at her, Shiro pretended she was his. Just before dawn, the birds began to sing from their cages in the nearby trees. He feigned sleep, watching through his eyelashes as she rose and dressed. Then she was gone.

– IV –

In which the master suffers a bore whose worst fear is realized

Marta Vélez agreed to resume relations with Rodrigo after he presented her with a gold necklace and promised to never mention her nephew again. One evening when he should have been returning to Sevilla, he conspired to remain in Madrid. He took his prospective son-in-law to dine with Miguel de Cervantes Saavedra.

Rodrigo had come to know Cervantes while the author was imprisoned in Sevilla. The Grandee had food and writing materials regularly sent to the jail, and due to his intercession, Cervantes was released a year earlier than his sentence decreed. Rodrigo had not acted out of compassion or literary fervor. The only books seen in his households were volumes dedicated to hunting, the Bible, and, for show, Francesco Guicciardini's *The History of Italy*. He had acted rather at the behest of his wife. Doña Inmaculada pointed out that the doctored accounts for which Cervantes had been unjustly imprisoned dated from a time when the writer worked as a purveyor of funds for the Spanish Armada. The admiral of the Armada was Rodrigo's great-uncle, the Duke of Medina-Sidonia.

Afterwards, Cervantes was always willing to show his gratitude, and recently, more than ever, in light of the fact that Rodrigo had become a close friend of the most powerful mortal breathing on the peninsula, the Duke of Lerma. Cervantes hated the Duke of Lerma. When the King showed favor toward the author and instructed the Duke to lend the writer a hand, he had only dispensed the meagerest of funds, forcing Cervantes into poverty. Worse still, a spurious 'continuation' of his *Quijote* had appeared in Tarragona that very year, written, he was sure, by one of the Duke of Lerma's minions, Fray Luis de Aliaga. The book had been a great success. But even with all of this, the last thing Cervantes wished was to end up on the Duke's bad side.

On that particular evening, after laboring all day on his own second part of *Don Quijote*, he was glad for any interruption, especially one that included an invitation to a sumptuous meal. The tavern where they dined, popular and lively, was found along the fashionable end of the Calle Mayor not far from where Cervantes lived. Ever since Phillip the Second chose Madrid over Valladolid as the permanent capital, thousands of courtiers and nobles and the people who provided for them had flocked to the city, tripling its population. The area around the Alcázar, the royal palace, built along a promontory above the narrow stream affectionately called the "River" Manzanares, had become a filthy warren of narrow streets. These dirtied lanes were relieved here and there by a number of modest plazas. The whole labyrinthine network was scalding in summer, damp and cold in the winter. As the *madrileños* were known to say about the climate of their city, '*Son seis meses de invierno y seis de infierno.*' (Six months of winter and six of hell.)

Over roasted lamb so succulent it could be sliced with the edge of a porcelain plate—a novelty the tiresome proprietor never wearied of demonstrating—and with the aid of a raw but pleasing red wine stored below in large clay cisterns, Rodrigo tried to impress his future son-in-law by pretending more familiarity with the writer than truth could admit.

'I live in an old-fashioned, provincial, overly ceremonious world, amigo,' he said to the author. 'But you who have seen and contemplated the mysteries of life on many shores and who live here in this ceaseless tangle of humanity, in this far harsher sphere, pray tell me and this young nobleman with us this evening, how do you view the behavior of today's youth?'

Cervantes was accustomed to the odd way in which Rodrigo spoke to him. Informed by other acquaintances that the Grandee was otherwise known for his directness, for being an elegant but taciturn man whose only known weaknesses were hunting, whoring, and his daughter, Cervantes had correctly concluded that the convoluted sentences Rodrigo used when speaking with him was the man's mangled attempt to emulate what he imagined to be literary conversation. It amused Cervantes and even inspired some compassion for a man he suspected was a brute at heart.

He also knew from previous evenings that Rodrigo fancied himself a kindred soul, a man of the world who had also tasted battle. Though this amused the writer some, it occasionally irritated him. For Cervantes had actually been a soldier, had been shot twice in the chest and once in his left arm during the battle of Lepanto. It was not for nothing he was called the *Manco de Lepanto*. Then he had spent five years captive in Algiers, from whose infested dungeons he had tried on numerous occasions to escape. Rodrigo, on the other hand, who regularly claimed to have seen active service during Spain's unsuccessful naval war with England in 1588, had been but an eighteen-year-old aide-de-camp to his great-uncle, the 7th Duke of Medina-Sidonia. Apart from a prolonged bout of seasickness, Rodrigo and his illustrious relation had survived the debacle without a scratch. While Cervantes sat in chains taunted by murderous jailers, Rodrigo and his uncle had continued a life of linen sheets at country estates rife with game, pious wives, and willing servant girls.

'I am not certain I grasp the exact meaning of your query,' Cervantes replied. 'But it seems to me that youths today comport themselves much like they always have.'

'Not at all, my friend,' Rodrigo said dismissively, 'At least among my class of people, and please do not take that the wrong way.'

'Not at all, Don Rodrigo.'

The irony of the repeated phrase was lost upon the aristocrat, but not upon the youth sitting next to him.

'When you and I were young we went to war, Miguel, and gladly,' Rodrigo said with an expression that implied he might actually be remembering scenes of gory battles barely survived. 'I've yet to meet or hear of any nobleman's son today who is eager to prove himself in a similar fashion.' This last phrase was accompanied by a gentle elbow aimed at Julian's ribs.

Cervantes did his best to appear interested and understanding, wondering where, if anywhere, the inane conversation was going. Simultaneously, he enjoyed a spasm of relief upon noticing that a short man entering the tavern he at first feared to be the rival he most maligned and detested, the insufferable and crowd-pleasing Lope de Vega, was in fact someone else.

'Where would you suggest these youth brandish their swords, Don Rodrigo? We've been at peace with the English since 1604 and with the Dutch for five years now.'

'None of that will last, my friend. Trust me on this, I who have the confidence of many in the know about these things. But that was not really my point. What I most fear with respect to our youth,' Rodrigo said, looking at the author with a seriousness that was almost comical, 'is an alarming rise in perversity.'

This caught the author's attention.

'Perversity.'

'Depraved perversity, young men cavorting with relatives rather than testing their mettle on the battlefield.'

Julian felt a blush rise up from his throat. Cervantes placed his good hand on Rodrigo's wrist.

'Tell me, good man. What is bothering you? When you say 'cavorting,' are you referring to carnal relations?'

Rodrigo emptied his goblet and closed his eyes for a moment.

'*Exactamente.*'

'This is the first I am hearing of such behavior. Perhaps it is only the case within your higher circles.'

Rodrigo, suddenly not in the mood for literary wit, responded with a grumbling noise and ordered more wine.

'But if that be so,' Cervantes persisted, 'I must say it would not constitute a novelty.'

'What in damnation are you referring to?' Rodrigo sputtered.

'What do you think, young man?' Cervantes asked Julian, ignoring the other man's fulminations in the hope of widening the forum.

'I confess,' Julian said, staring down at the surface of the table stained with grease, 'I've little notion of what this is all about.'

'Well, I should hope not,' Rodrigo said, a bit too energetically.

Cervantes wondered whether a form of ictus might be in play.

'What I am referring to, sir,' the writer said, 'is a phenomenon common throughout history, so much so I see little point in devoting more time to it.'

'Common? Common you say?' Rodrigo fumed.

'Common in your decidedly uncommon upper classes.'

'Damn you man! This is not what I wished for you to say.'

All three men took stock of this latter declaration with varying degrees of puzzlement.

'Our own king was married to his cousin,' Cervantes said. 'The Hapsburg Monarch Maximillian II married *his* first cousin, María of Spain, daughter of Charles the Fifth, and they had sixteen children. Cleopatra was married to her younger brother. Adonis was the child of a father and his daughter. Abraham and his wife Sarah were half-siblings. Brother and sister unions were common during the Roman period. Though an aura of taboo has often accompanied this sort of cavorting, as you call it, the practice it seems is as old and "common" as man himself.'

'What utter nonsense,' Rodrigo said.

'I find it fascinating,' said the young man.

'Do you believe in the Bible, Don Rodrigo?' Cervantes asked.

'Well, of course I do.'

'Who did Cain have his children with? The only woman about was Eve, his mother. So we are all descended from carnal relations between relatives, sir.'

Rodrigo finished his meal in a foul temper, wondering if there might be a way to have the famous author brought before the Holy Office of the Inquisition. As they left the premises, he was set upon by Gaspar de Guzmán with his absurd moustache, the fawning nephew of Don Baltasar de Zúñiga. Gaspar de Guzmán spent his time laboring to ingratiate himself with the young prince who would someday become King Philip the Fourth, just as the Duke of Lerma had with the prince's father. Finally disentangled from the smoke-filled tavern after repeated exchanges of pointless backslapping, the three men said good-bye out front. Cervantes gave Julian a wink and told him to take good care of his future father-in-law. Rodrigo made a heroic effort to overcome his bad humor and bid the author adieu with admirable grace, if only because the moment he had been waiting for all evening was fast at hand.

As an awkward silence enveloped them, the aristocrats watched Cervantes walk off, the lame arm hanging limply at his side, his posture stooped. There then ensued a brief roundelay about who should accompany whom back to their lodgings. Julian insisted upon seeing Don Rodrigo to the room prepared for him at the Alcázar, and the latter thought it wisest to accede. During the ten minutes it took them to reach the Royal Palace and doing their best to ignore the appalling scent in the air from the garbage and human waste lining the gutters, they took turns extolling the virtues of Guada. After passing through the guarded gates, they embraced and said good-night. But less than a minute later, Rodrigo was pursuing the young man back through the dark streets, a hunter stalking his buck. Part of him desperately hoped the boy would go to the *Academia de Madrid* that, over dinner, the youth had casually mentioned as the place where he was staying, but Rodrigo was prepared for the worst.

And thus it was. The boy went straight to the palacete of his aunt, built along the Carrer de San Geronimo, where the Duke of Lerma kept a residence as well. Following the fashion, these large buildings had austere windows and balconies and facades made of simple brick, but they hid sumptuous, colorful interiors filled with paintings and French furniture. Rodrigo watched as Julian let himself in with the relaxed assurance of someone well accustomed to being welcomed there. Feeling like a buffoon and praying he would not be seen or caught or fall and break his head, the forty-eight-year-old Grandee of Spain climbed a plantain tree outside the window of Marta's bedroom and found a perch with an ideal view through her windows.

Were it not for the emotions shredding his heart he would have been most pleased with the privileged view he achieved, a voyeur's dream. Enough candles were lit within to permit him to suffer the entire reunion: the torrid embrace, the mad kisses, the mutual disrobing, the sickeningly intimate caresses thereafter, seeing her do something to the young nephew she had never done to him, and then, upon the bed he had left that very morning, the culminating act during which his Marta uttered moans and cries far more intense than any he had ever inspired. It took more control than he was used to not to cry out himself. As he began to clamber back down, numbed with despair, he heard them laughing, swept up in postcoital joy. He would have wagered Guada's dowry they were laughing at his expense.

Rodrigo returned to the Alcázar a wounded beast, feeling his age, immensely sorry for himself while manufacturing outrage for his poor deluded daughter. He'd been reduced to the cuckolded fool the Duke of Lerma had called him. Sleep did not come easily as he moped about the royal apartment, the one where his wife always pictured him, but where he rarely ever stayed. What was a man like himself to do, he thought? It was expected he have a mistress. Now he would have to seek another, a task that night that felt Herculean. How could Marta be so treacherous? For the past five years, he had made her life infinitely more comfortable than it would have been. Was he that boring, that dull in bed, that pompous and ridiculous?

– V –

In which tea is prepared and the journey begins -A hand is lost and a friend secured

Before departing Sendai, Shiro was called to tea by his mother. It was just the two of them and the monk who performed the ceremony. Keeping his head bowed, the monk used leaves that were direct descendants of those brought from China by Eisai at the end of the 12th century. Once concluded and with the humble officiate paid and gone, mother and son remained.

'We may never see each other again,' Mizuki said, looking into her son's eyes.

Shiro smiled. 'Two years is not such a long a time, and you are still young and beautiful.'

Mizuki gazed down at the bamboo mat she knelt upon. She did not return his smile.

'My husband was young and beautiful, like you, and died that way. My closest friend, Kókiko, tripped when she was fifteen, cut her knee, and was dead a week later from infection.'

'Your husband died in battle,' Shiro replied. 'I go on a mission of peace. Your friend may have been clumsy, while I am sure of foot, and you are a portrait of grace.'

'I did not ask you here to listen to flattery,' she said. 'You know of what I speak, the precariousness of life, the distances you will be traveling, the inherent danger for you. Hasekura Tsunenari is

27

known for his greed, his son Hasekura Tsunenaga for his envy. Everyone knows whose sword you carry.'

'The Lord thinks otherwise.'

'The Lord is sometimes naive.'

Besides the mother of Date Masamune's children, no one, Shiro knew, could speak of the Lord in such a manner.

'I will keep your counsel in mind, mother.'

'I worry about you,' she said, softening.

'There is no need to.'

'Of course there is. And I regret sometimes the path assigned to you.'

'The path?'

'The Warrior's Way.'

'It is a great honor to follow it.'

She reached out to him, for the first time in many years, taking his right hand and kissing his sixth finger, the flesh of her flesh. He was part of her, made from her. The size and strength of him there next to her only served to reveal the chasm of time that had opened since the day of his birth. He had belonged to her.

'It is said that we come into the world alone and alone we leave it,' she said.

'It is a guiding truth,' he replied.

'But it is a lie,' she said. 'When you came into this world, I was with you, you were attached to me. We were together. My fear, my terror, is that we shall leave this world without each other.'

'If I promise to return, then you must promise not to fall ill, or trip upon the ground.'

She smiled and let him go.

'I promise,' she said.

'Then you have my word as well,' he said.

'Here,' she said, reaching into a fold of her kimono. 'I want you to take this with you.'

She handed him a small envelope.

'*Biwa* seeds,' she said, 'that my mother gave to me. Keep them with you, and we can plant them together upon your return.'

He took the envelope from her and bowed.

She noticed that a peony the monk had leaned to the side in the small vase next to his utensils contained a beetle that slowly made its way within the pink petals. She wondered what the room would look like were she its size, suspended within the glowing hue.

'One more thing,' she said to her son. 'Try and not be lonely, try to love your loneliness, do not let it go, treasure it with all your heart.'

***

The ship was called the Date Maru. It set sail in the ninth month of the Christian year 1613 from Toshima-Tsukinoura. Mizuki cried all the day and night before. Lord Masamune saw the ship off, mounted on his horse. He watched from the harbor's end as the vessel transformed from a large and colorful artifice of planks, masts, and shouting men into an ephemeral speck that disappeared from the edge of the horizon.

Conditions aboard were trying, even for the privileged Samurai. One hundred and eighty-two men on a vessel that size left little to the imagination. Early on, Shiro found a place on deck midship where he would spend long hours meditating, sharpening his sword, and gazing at the sea. It was a novelty he did not tire of. He preferred the view from the bowsprit, but it was there all aboard went to relieve themselves. He made himself useful, shunned special treatment, and did his best to adapt. The land you stand upon, he thought, the sea you fall through. A house kept one steady and private, a ship never ceased moving, and everywhere you turned there was someone an arm's length away. Men fierce in battle vomited beside skinny merchants whose only use for a blade was to cut bread.

He noticed that Father Sotelo never got ill. The hawk-faced priest appeared especially energized by the voyage and often sought the ear of Hasekura Tsunenaga. Sotelo's friars who accompanied him proselytized to a captive audience in a manner the young Samurai found unbecoming.

Through his own sources, Hasekura Tsunenaga had learned of the high esteem Shiro was held in by the Date Masamune. He also knew Shiro to be a bastard and thus, he believed, someone to be disparaged. During the first two weeks of the voyage, neither made any attempt to address the other, until one day, walking about the deck with his retainers, Hasekura Tsunenaga found the young Samurai alone at his station. They bowed to each other, Shiro prolonging his respectfully.

'What is your name, young man?' Hasekura Tsunenaga asked, knowing full well the answer.

'I am called Shiro, my captain.'

'You are with the Sendai Samurai.'

'Yes, sir.'

'And how do you find the voyage thus far?'

'Most wondrous sir.'

'I quite agree. But have you any complaints?'

'No sir – or – perhaps one.'

'And what might that be?'

After asking this question, he made the slightest of gestures toward the men with him, as if to say, what is one to make of the bastard's cheek?

'I am troubled,' Shiro said, noting the gesture but seeing no path of retreat, 'by the unsupervised contact between us and the barbarians.'

'To what are you referring?'

'To the unsolicited barbarian preaching.'

'And what would you propose?'

'Discipline my captain, segregation, mutual respect, our customary codes of conduct.'

'You seem to forget, Shiro-san, the sole purpose of this voyage as dictated by your own Lord.'

Shiro could see the man would try to humiliate him and that he had erred in being forthright, but being young, he felt anger rising within. He wished to point out that Date Masamune was Hasekura Tsunenaga's Lord as well, and the man who had pardoned Hasekura Tsunenaga's life.

'With great and due respect,' Shiro said, 'I have not forgotten. It is just that I feel the more we maintain our own way of life, even in these crowded circumstances, the more the barbarians will respect us, those aboard, and most important, those we shall meet across the great seas.'

The retainers raised their eyebrows, tensed their hands about the hilts of their swords. They had never heard a Samurai of Shiro's rank address Hasekura Tsunenaga in this manner.

'As the leading member of a noble family, I prefer to hear advice from my equals, Shiro-san.'

'I was only answering your question. I regret saying anything you might find offensive.'

'No harm done. And now I know better than to ask again.'

He made as if to continue with his inspection about the deck of the ship, but then he paused and added one more thing as Shiro remained bowed before him.

'It will be a special pleasure when, reaching New Spain, I shall watch your baptism into the barbarian faith.'

Alarmed, Shiro knew better than to reveal it. He kept his head down and remained quiet until Hasekura Tsunenaga and his men moved on. Rumor of these baptisms had spread amongst the Sendai Samurai, but they had deemed it to be malicious gossip.

In the midst of a weeklong storm, a silk tradesman from Edo was lost overboard, a death Shiro could not erase from his mind. The brutal happenstance, the loneliness of it, the terror. After a month at sea, they moored off an island that had a stream they used to bathe in and to replenish their water supply. They drank coconut milk. Archers hunted birds. Shiro taught himself to swim. A week later en route again, sixty-three whales surrounded them. At night, awaiting sleep, Shiro contemplated what William Adams had called the *Via Lactea*, feeling unique and trivial in the same instant.

One day he overheard a Spaniard making fun of Father Sotelo. Though the young Samurai was grateful to the priest for all he had learned, he considered the man too proud, too enamored of young boys, and excessively fired up with Christian fervor. The offending Spaniard was from Sevilla and called Diego. He was aghast when Shiro addressed him in Spanish. From then on, they took their evening meals together.

'Each day you get closer to your home, and I farther away from mine,' Shiro said one evening when there was still light enough to observe a school of dolphins racing ahead of the ship.

'You will return to Sendai one day, my friend, and have adventures and tales to tell for a lifetime,' Diego replied.

'That is difficult for me to imagine.'

'As it was for me when I set off from Sanlúcar three years past.'

There came a week of humid weather and doldrums when the ship went nowhere and tempers frayed. Diego tripped over a dozing Samurai loyal to the Shogun Tokugawa Ieyasu, and an argument ensued that quickly escalated. They began to curse each other, raising the ante, spewing epithets neither understood the meaning of. When Diego made the fateful decision to pull out his dagger—so enraged did he become at the bullying gibberish spit his way—the Samurai drew his sword and in one stroke severed the Spaniard's knife hand from the rest of him. A geyser of blood shot forth. Everyone cried out and gathered around the two men in a circle. Diego fell to his knees staring at his wound in horror as the offended Samurai raised his sword with both hands to finish him off. It was then that Shiro broke through the circle to deflect the blow with the sword given to him by Date Masamune. His attempts to calm his unhinged colleague failed, for the Samurai insisted on more blood. As another Spaniard pulled Diego to safety, staunching the wound with the shirt off his back, the rest of the men looked on in thrilled fascination at the dueling warriors. The aggressor was gruff, experienced, and massive, Shiro, who had never fought in battle, lean and poised.

In five classic strokes executed with a degree of precision that would be much commented upon, Shiro disarmed the older man, knocking the sword from his hand and sending it out over the water. The Shogun's Samurai, humiliated beyond repair, bowed to Shiro, went to his knees, and, before anyone could stop him, drew his Tanto blade and spilled his bowels upon the already bloodstained deck. Hasekura Tsunenaga reached the scene furious. He feared for a riot and feared even more that the young Samurai would be revered for his decisive intercession.

Diego was cared for but almost died from fever after his stump was cauterized. Whatever sympathy Father Sotelo had gained among the Samurai with his teachings evaporated the instant he explained how their colleague's soul would now burn in the Christian hell-fires for all eternity because of his suicide. Shiro was detained and brought to the captain's cabin after three days of being locked below without food or drink.

'What have you to say for yourself?' Hasekura Tsunenaga asked him.

'Would you rather the Samurai from Edo had beheaded the barbarian?' Shiro replied quietly.

'How dare you speak to me like that?'

'How dare you imprison me with no cause?'

'I have kept you from the Edo Samurais' revenge.'

'You have kept me without food or drink. The Edo Samurai, like the Sendai Samurai, follow the Warrior's Way. There is no cause for revenge.'

'I thought you were for remaining apart from the barbarians.'

'I had no choice in the matter.'

'And yet no one else intervened.'

The cabin had a window, and through it Shiro could see the ocean, calm that day, dark and purple as eggplant. Hasekura Tsunenaga continued.

34

'There is only one representative of Date Masamune in this Delegation, and that is I. I speak with his voice. I represent and shall intercede for his interests. You are nothing but a bastard boy tolerated at his whim.'

His retainers believed Hasekura Tsunenaga had acted out of weakness, that punishing the young Samurai would only tarnish his own authority, that the correct course would have been to praise Shiro and commend his actions. But they did not say so. He was returned to the deck but without his sword, for Hasekura Tsunenaga coveted it. The Samurai from both houses welcomed the young man and commiserated with him. Diego regretted his fit of anger and thanked Shiro for saving his life. Father Sotelo and the other priests shunned the young man. Shiro felt changed. The first real sword fight of his life and the three days of imprisonment had toughened him. Stripping and gripping a line, he let himself be dragged through the sea, letting the cold salt water cleanse and refresh him.

A week later gulls visited the ship, and as it emerged from a thick mist one morning that lay low upon the water, they found themselves a hundred yards off a rocky beach of what would one day be called the Monterey Peninsula. It was part of the land Spanish explorers had named 'California,' after the imaginary paradise described in Garci de Rodríguez Montalvo's book *Las Sergas de Esplandián*. The Date Maru came about and tacked south, hugging the coast. Several hours later, it finally dropped anchor at the small, protected cove of San Simeon.

In which naïveté becomes a burden

Doña Soledad Medina y Pérez Guzman de la Cerda became a widow at the age of thirty when her fifty-four-year-old husband perished from a heart attack while ravishing the plump fourteen-year-old daughter of his game warden. The fortune Doña Soledad inherited, when added to her own, made her one of the wealthiest women in Europe. After a failed love affair with her cousin, the Duke of Medina-Sidonia, she took on one more lover, the priest, another cousin once removed, who had baptized and buried her sons. But on the occasion of her forty-second saint's day, Doña Soledad's chambermaid informed her that the priest had been heard having relations with the cook's younger sister. She paid the cook handsomely to have the priest poisoned and never went to bed with another man. It was around this time, seeking to fulfill a long buried and much frustrated desire for a daughter, that she transferred all her remaining affections to her niece, Guada.

When Don Rodrigo returned to Sevilla and confirmed the news concerning Julian's relationship with Marta Vélez, Doña Soledad was present. She had known for some time about Rodrigo's long-term dalliance with the Vélez woman, as well, but she had never whispered a hint of it to Doña Inmaculada. She never liked the idea of Julian Gutiérrez y González marrying her favorite niece. She considered his family, despite claims to old blood and significant properties, inappropriate for the prized maidenhead of a singular Medinaceli. As she listened to Rodrigo's declaration that day and comforted Inmaculada afterwards, she swore an oath to herself to try and, somehow, set things right.

A month before the wedding, she had Guada to lunch. They sat at a small table in a private dining room adjacent to the lesser of Soledad's two gardens. The young girl was beautiful, as beautiful as she herself had once been, and as they ate two platefuls of delicate baby shrimp, shells and all, washed down with a chilled Manzanilla wine from one of her many bodegas, the older woman came straight to the point.

'May we speak in absolute confidence, my dear?'

'Of course.'

'Your parents have discovered something unpleasant concerning Julian, and as they are too ashamed to speak with you about it, they have placed their trust in me.'

'Are you being serious, aunt?'

'Quite serious, my dear.'

'What sort of unpleasantness?' the young girl asked.

'It seems he has a mistress.'

'You mean his aunt, Marta Vélez?'

'Good god girl, do you know about it?'

'I've known for as long as we've been betrothed.'

'I don't know what to say. Do you approve of such a thing?'

'How could I? But I've been grateful for his honesty. We've argued about it on many occasions, and he has promised me, for some time now, that once we marry he shall not see her again.'

Soledad wondered whether the girl also knew about her father's entanglement with the woman but thought it best not to ask.

'You amaze me,' she said. 'I had no idea you were capable of such *sangfroid*.'

'I don't know what it is. I only know that I love him and that was part of him when we became engaged. What is more unpleasant for me is that my parents and you know of it.'

Soledad finished her drink and took out her fan, opening it with an expert flick of the wrist.

'Do not concern yourself about that, my dear. Leave it to me. If, as you say, you love the boy in spite of this, then that is sufficient. The reason I invited you here was to see if you still wished to carry through with the wedding, but I see the answer is yes.'

'Absolutely yes.'

'And you think he will do as he promised?'

'To stay with a woman as old as she, once he has me all to himself, is inconceivable.'

Ah, thought her aunt, and just when I was about to congratulate her for her maturity.

'And you get along well.'

'We get along splendidly.'

'And you are not consumed with jealousy?'

'Yes I am. But what am I supposed to do? My own father has other women. Your husband had other women. They say even our pious King has other women. Why should it be otherwise for Julian?'

Soledad considered her niece anew, for now the girl was again demonstrating a sagacity beyond her years.

'That a couple might end up that way is one thing, dear,' she said, closing the fan. 'But that a marriage begin in such a manner, when the two of you are so young, is something else.'

'He's told me he will stop seeing her. To give him up a priori feels very harsh, absurd.'

Soledad raised a hand to her mouth, a tic she resorted to when faced with doubt. Her fingertips smelled of the shrimp, of the damp sands of Cádiz. She rinsed them in a small silver bowl by her plate filled with water and slices of lemon.

'Has he kissed you?' her aunt asked.

'No.'

'Has he tried?'

'Of course he has, along with many other things. But I have forbidden it, until. . .'

'Poor girl.'

'To tell you the truth I am more concerned about what will happen on our wedding night than I am about what he does with his ugly aunt.'

'Worried, or intrigued?'

'I have no experience, and it seems he has more than enough.'

The delicate girl paused. Out through the open doors giving on to the patio, she watched two birds bathing in the shallow upper tier of the fountain, flapping their wings. 'But then I think, even if that part of our life proves unsatisfactory, how important is it in the end? Is not the fact we are suited for each other in so many ways more important than what goes on in the night?'

'You are too young for this sort of wisdom, dear. You've no cause to think that "what goes on in the night" shall be a disappointment.'

'I shall just have to see. Mother was not encouraging, though she and father are still together and civil with each other, when that aspect of their lives has been an absolute disaster.'

'And yet you are here, thank god, because of them.'

On her way home, Guada did the crying she prevented herself from giving into in front of her aunt. Once she collected herself, she instructed the coachman to steer the carriage down by the water's edge. Stepping gingerly, protected from the sun with a dainty umbrella brought from Paris years past by her aunt's deceased husband, she walked to where the earth began to soften and stared at the Guadalquivir. The river was alive with light and motion. The noise from its flow was a comfort to her. Its name came from the Arabic al-wādi al-kabīr, الوادي الكبير, 'The Great River.' The Phoenicians before them had named it the *Baits*, and later *Betis* or *Baetis*, giving its name to the Roman province *Hispania Baetica*. An older Celtiberian name was *Oba*, meaning river of gold.

Its golden patina held forth that afternoon. Hidden beneath the moving surface swam trout, barbel, black bass, sturgeon, pike, and carp. She closed her eyes and smelled it and gave thanks to her father, with all his faults, for the folly of having her baptized in its waters.

– VII –

In which the travelers reach the New World

A rookery of ungainly, full-whiskered elephant seals basked along the curved briny beach betwixt dried strands of kelp and seaweed on San Simeon Bay. The morning mist had burned off by noon, and a gentle December sun warmed their tawny hides. The Samurais watched, indifferent some of them, others appalled, as a high-spirited cadre of Spanish sailors went about shooting the animals at close range with their muskets. By the time enough of the herd had sensed the danger and returned to the safety of the sea, loudly lumbering into the meager waves, at least thirty of their brethren lay behind bleeding to death.

The barbarians claimed the meat to be excellent and the blubber useful, the skins ideal for winter garments. But the vast number of dying beasts made it plain to most that the killing had taken place for its own sake.

Shiro and Diego, not participants in this spectacle, walked inland a good hour away from the shore, inspired by a simple need to get away from the rest and feel the assurance of solid ground beneath their feet. They made their way through green fields of long grass and tarweed, through small groves of twisted live oak, cypress, and cedars bent by winds. A family of deer grazed upon a distant hill dotted with junipers and Monterey pines. As they looked further east, higher hills rose in succession. The smell of the land raised their spirits.

Shiro asked Diego if Father Sotelo was well known in Sevilla.

'The general impression we have of him is that he is trying to make a name for himself, an ambition that, in Sevilla, was thwarted. Thus, like myself, he has looked to gain some success by going abroad. The order to which he belongs, the Franciscans, is a rival of the Jesuits. Not wealthy or influential enough to rise to the rank of Bishop or Cardinal in Spain or in Rome, priests like him look to distinguish themselves preaching in new territories where, if enough converts enter the Church, they might someday be named Archbishop of distant flocks.'

'But do they actually believe in what they preach? The man on the cross who is also god, one of three including a dove that is also just one god, the idea of heaven and hell?'

Diego grinned, for he had never considered his religion from a foreigner's view. 'What,' he asked the Samurai, 'do you believe in?'

'In very little. In the power of nothing. The brevity of life, the simplicity of earth and stone.'

'Well,' Diego rejoined, incapable of commenting on this blasphemous stance, 'many of the priests do believe in our religion, and many just pretend to, or, better put, they use it toward their own ends. It is hard to know in Sotelo's case. Many priests are second or third sons who, unable to inherit a sufficient amount of their family's wealth, take their vows as a practical and socially condoned alternative. Which explains why there is so much hypocrisy: priests who fornicate, priests with mistresses and children, Cardinals, even the Pope.'

'Men are men,' Shiro said, 'the world over.'

'Now there's a sharp shard of truth,' Diego agreed.

'I cannot imagine Father Sotelo with a woman, though perhaps he has one waiting for him in Spain. In Japan, what he most seemed to enjoy was looking at the men in the baths.'

Diego laughed. They paused, took stock of how far they had strayed from the bay, turned, and began to retrace their steps. The ship, seen from that distance, presented an elegant composition anchored in the pristine water, surrounded by such an array of untrammeled nature. Rather than head back to the clearing where the beach was, littered now with the giant dead seals being assaulted by fleas and flies, they set a course for a modest peninsula or *Cerro* that formed the bay's northern promontory of protection, an advancement of land rich in shade from towering eucalyptus trees.

'How about you?' Diego asked. 'Have you left someone special behind?'

Shiro recalled his day and night with Yokiko, the peach scent that hovered about her skin, her shy smile, the sounds she made with him in the darkness.

'No,' he said, 'except for my mother. There was someone. But she is not waiting for my return.'

'So you are a free man. Perhaps you'll find a Spanish or an Italian girl.'

'Perhaps,' said the young Samurai, to be polite. 'Though I prefer my own kind.'

'Have it your way,' said the Spaniard, never unaware for long of the stark differences between them.

'And you?' Shiro asked. 'Who is counting the weeks until your return?'

'Aye, there is someone,' Diego said. 'A young woman I am engaged to marry. But I worry that after so much time her heart may have chilled. And when she sees this,' he added, raising his stump aloft, 'only God knows how far she shall run.'

Nevertheless, Shiro envied the Christian.

By the time they reached the woods of the promontory, they could see the longboats returning to the ship, the sails being readied, and heard the bell summoning everyone aboard. Rather than walk back toward the beach, they made their way down to the rocks, stripped and tied their garments tight, and waded into the cold water, pushing aside swaths, green, rubbery kelp entangled with soggy strips of eucalyptus bark. They swam to the ship directly, Diego making admirable progress with the use of a single arm. Within the hour, the Date Maru had left the bay and resumed its heading south toward New Spain.

– VIII –

In which nature bestows a gift

Julian and Guada lay side by side in the shade. The Moorish tiles under them, littered with fallen blossoms, covered the surface of an expansive terrace. An open pair of tall glass doors behind them connected the terrace to a master bedroom. They had arrived at the estate an hour earlier and were still formally attired. After four days and nights of the social fury surrounding their wedding, they were relieved to be alone.

When they closed their eyes, their ears focused on the rustling leaves, the waterspouts feeding the garden fountains below, the cries of darting swallows. Opening their eyes revealed a twilight sky and the swallows racing through it, hithering and thithering, turning and swooping, rising and falling, the sharp little wings catching remnants of a setting sun only birds could see.

The raspberry-hued thirty-five-room finca at La Moratalla belonged to her aunt, Soledad Medina. Though Andalusian at heart, the main house had been repainted and decorated a century earlier by a duchess from Gascoigne who had married into the family. It sat in rural grandeur hidden by towering palms and plantains, flanked by well-tended gardens, graveled paths, and groves of orange trees rarely harvested. The outside world was kept at bay by ivy-covered walls barely visible in the distance and an imposing wrought iron gate emblazoned with the Medinaceli coat of arms. Apart from the live-in servants responsible for meals and maintenance, and the day laborers who arrived by mule each morning from Palma del Río, the newlyweds had the estate to themselves.

When the option to stay there was first proposed, Julian had wavered. His first inclination was to organize a house party, a continuance of the wedding feast, inviting a coterie of friends to Carmona or Madrid. His concept of a good time had much to do with drinking surrounded by male friends and little to do with intimacy. But a conversation with Guada a week before the ceremony had changed his mind. Shortly before they were to enter the eating hall at Doña Soledad's palace in Sevilla where the table was set for twenty-two, Guada had taken him aside.

'I have not failed to notice the clouds darkening your spirit,' she said. 'I think I know their source.'

'I do not know of what you speak,' he said.

But the irises of her eyes, green like sea pebbles, and her dark brown pupils bore into him. 'I'm reminded of how the Guadalquivir begins as a trickle in the forests of Cazorla, and then how it transforms moving west, league by league, widening and deepening into the waterway gracing my city.'

'What, my dear, are you getting at?'

He tried to hide his impatience. Her throat reddened the way it did when she became upset.

'I only mean I would be most pained should your anxieties deepen as the altar approaches.'

He began to interrupt her, 'Guada. . .'

'Let me say just one thing, Julian. I marry you freely, you as you are. We have known each other since childhood, and I have come to care for your heart, your heart with all its complications and extraneous attachments. Nothing else matters. Trust me, and you shall see of what I speak.'

As the ensuing meal progressed, he felt a weight lift from him, and his admiration for her grew.

And now they were married as evening enveloped the Moratalla estate. The tiles cooled. The orange blossoms began to secrete their aroma into the evening air. The swallows dispersed, the fruit bats arrived.

'Come to bed,' she said.

They lit no tapers or candles. The house, rarely occupied, and even the silken threads of the bedspread disbursed a liturgical odor of beeswax and breviaries, tabernacular dampness and old wooden pew.

– IX –

In which a warning is offered

A clean Pacific breeze flattened the azure surface of Acapulco Bay. The Date Maru, rechristened by the barbarians as the San Juan Bautista, lay at anchor. Its timbers creaked. Its hull gathered barnacles. The ship and its cabins were empty save for some cats and a musket-bearing sailor standing guard.

In town, the Spanish colonial authorities had greeted the Japanese with fanfare. But within a week, they relieved the Samurai of their weapons, except for those of Hasekura Tsunenaga and his closest bodyguards. An absurd altercation over gifts and protocol had left two Spaniards wounded. The Japanese found their hosts malodorous and unpredictable. But the local populace continued to marvel at the Japanese mode of dress, the bolts of silk offered in trade, their use of chopsticks instead of forks or fingers.

After two months of rudimentary religious instruction and classes for the Samurai to try and learn Spanish, the next phase of their journey got under way. Hasekura Tsunenaga ordered a delegation of traders from Edo to stay in Acapulco, but the rest and all of the Samurai set out for Mexico City by way of Chilpancingo and Cuernavaca. It was April in the capital when they arrived, and they were greeted with crowds and fiestas. Hasekura Tsunenaga ordered the first baptisms to take place. Archbishop Don Juan Pérez de la Serna supervised the rites personally, and a large congregation looked on as the Samurai including Shiro were admitted into the Holy Roman Apostolic faith. The Samurai obeyed out of fealty and politeness. Only a handful had begun to take the priests seriously. The joke going round in private among the warriors was that being baptized was the only way to ensure getting a bath.

Hasekura Tsunenaga took up residence at the finca of the Spanish governor. Many of the Samurai were housed at local military barracks. But some, including Shiro, guided by his friend Diego, found rooms at a brothel, where baths were arranged and where women provided services in exchange for silk. The women came to call Shiro 'Tlazopilli,' Aztec for 'the handsome noble,' for how he was formed and carried himself. While the other Samurai staying there indulged in the new surroundings and grew lazy swallowing inordinate amounts of spicy food and spirits, Shiro followed the austere regimen practiced by those confined to the barracks.

Talking to the women and spending more time with Diego, he learned the story of how Mexico had been before the barbarians came, and how the generation of the women's grandparents had been subjugated. The brutality in the tales did not shock him, for the stories his mother and Katakura Kojuro and Date Masamune had told him of famous battles past had been equally gory. What affected him more was what one of the women said to him late one evening after all the rest had fallen asleep.

'Now they have come for your people,' she said. 'They start with smiles and promises, with their priests and crosses and holy water, speaking of trade and the brotherhood of nations. But none of it is true. At heart they are conquerors and thieves. You should turn back and save yourself. You should not go any further with them.'

'Diego will protect me while I am there.'

'Diego is just one man, and they are many thousands. And even Diego, if he has to, will choose his own kind over yours.'

They were joined in the capital by a Spanish Admiral, Don Antonio Oquendo, who, with a unit of soldiers wearing metal helmets and armed with muskets slung from their shoulders, led the embassy expedition from Mexico City down through Puebla and on to the port of Veracruz on the Gulf. A small fleet awaited them. Shortly after their arrival, their katana swords and tanto short knives confiscated in Acapulco were returned to the Samurai. Among them, its scabbard wrapped in canvas, was the sword given to Shiro by Date Masamune. He wondered whether it represented a peace offering, or something else. He examined it for damage, and while the others went on a three-day debauchery bidding farewell to Mexico, he remained near the harbor, fasting and sharpening his blade.

On the tenth of June, they were back on the water. He stood once more at the midship of a Spanish ship called the San José. The waters of the Gulf were crystalline. Immense turtles paddled close to the sandy sea floor. Under the command of Antonio Oquendo with Hasekura Tsunenaga at his side, the ship put Veracruz behind them and set a course for Cuba.

In which the Admiral of the High Seas recalls a painful day

Alonso Pérez de Guzmán y de Zúñiga-Sotomayor, the 7th Duke of Medina-Sidonia, observed the newlyweds from a balcony at his ancestral palace set in the hills outside the village of Medina-Sidonia. He tried, with the aid of a cane, to find a position in which the shooting pains in his hip might diminish. A light September drizzle fell. The couple in the garden below, recently arrived from La Moratalla, sat by the fountain holding hands. It irked him to see them oblivious to the weather. The beauty of his niece brought back memories of the first months he had spent with his own wife, Ana de Silva y Mendoza, the daughter of the Princess of Éboli. They were betrothed when the girl was only four and he fifteen. Eight years later, after a dispensation from the Pope due to Ana's age, they married. Now their children were grown and married, and the skinny girl who had been his twelve-year-old bride was long dead and buried in his family crypt not a five-minute walk from where he stood. He imagined her, shriveled and blackened, her rotting fingers covered in white gloves and rosary beads.

Inside, on his desk, there was a letter addressed to the *Admiral of the High Seas*, penned no doubt by an official in Sevilla looking to flatter, but who was unaware of how much the title irked him. Fellow nobles who knew him well had, at his request, ceased using the accolade years ago.

For reasons the Duke could never fathom, Philip the Second had handed him the helm of the Spanish Armada when the Marques of Santa Cruz died. He had refused, ineffectively, for he had no experience at sea. The ignominious defeat in 1588 at the hands of the English off the coast of France and Ireland was blamed on him. The sacking of Cádiz in 1596 had been blamed on him. Then they blamed his stubbornness in 1606 for the loss of a squadron of ships off the coast of Gibraltar. He always contended that the King, now deceased, had been a fool to choose him. The Duke was a Grandee of the land, a Duke at home on horseback riding through the countryside of his estates or along his family's beaches in Sanlúcar. He was a man of saddles and reins, dogs and hunting muskets. Sails and swirling seawater, ocean gales and slimy fish were alien to him. Oquendos and Bazanes were born and raised for that. He had not been bred to vomit over the side of a galleon or to issue orders to insolent sailors from Lugo. He could never live down the public humiliation the title had brought upon him.

And yet, he thought, the contents of the letter were curious and had a certain *gracia* about them. It claimed that a tribe of Asian devils was approaching Spain accompanied by Franciscans from Sevilla and a naval captain by the name of Sebastian Vizcaino, whose name was somehow familiar. The Asians had discovered the truth of Jesus Christ and sought trade. They came from an island nation he remembered being told about one evening some years back at a dinner where he was seated next to a Jesuit with knowledge of the subject. He remembered how the Jesuit told him that before the heathens of that land came to know Christianity, they had worshipped rocks and trees.

Let them come, he thought. Spain was hungry for new ports as well, new minerals and forests, new converts, new money. It was, after all, their holy obligation as soldiers for Christ. The letter implored him to organize a proper reception for the delegation. It went on to mention that most of the group had been baptized and that the nation they represented was known for its fine arts and exquisite manners.

He found the matter immensely ironic. Just when the issue of the purity of one's blood was being so hotly argued, prosecuted, and persecuted by a Holy Inquisition engorged with its own power, when its irons of torture were burning brightest, when only five years had passed since the new King and his disagreeable, *arriviste* sidekick, the Duke of Lerma, had expelled all of the Moriscos from Spain, just when all this was afoot, he was being asked to unfurl a carpet of welcome to another race of dubious converts. The Duke of Lerma, a thorn he could not remove, whose daughter was married to his oldest son Juan Mañuel who would succeed him someday and become the 8th Duke of Medina-Sidonia. He had given the pair his blessing in a moment of weakness.

He decided he would show the visitors from Japan and the palace officials asking him to greet them how an old aristocrat responds in times tainted by religious provincialism. He would open the palace in Sanlúcar de Barrameda and have all available carriages dusted and repainted and properly paired with braided steeds to meet and escort the tree-worshippers from their ship. It went without saying he would not be there to receive them in person. There were limits to be respected. He would send Julian, plus a nephew or two, to represent him. It would be a pleasure to have his niece to himself for a spell without the presence of the handsome young husband.

The pain in his hip continued as he made his way downstairs to his secretary's quarters. He dictated a response to Sevilla and to Madrid. He composed a separate and detailed letter to his man in Sanlúcar listing all the necessary preparations he could think of for the Asian delegation. He also commended the services of Don Julian and two ne'er-do-well nephews.

Afterwards he took a strong drink of wine and limped to the stables. As if to further affirm his ties to the land and putting up with considerable discomfort, he mounted his favorite Arabian and went for a ride up into the hills. He rode between hundreds of olive and almond trees. The paths were damp from the early morning rain. From earth the color of dried blood, there rose an odor of renewal, a scent of chthonic gratitude, primary odors the land awards to riders and horses fortunate enough to be out after a long-needed shower. He passed a family of *campesinos* harvesting potatoes and deigned to recognize their salutations with a brief wave while wistfully entertaining a fantasy he would have been happier born into a family such as theirs. He thought of his mistress from the village, Rosario, whom he had brought into the house to serve as Guada's chambermaid so that it would be easier to sneak her into his bedroom.

He reached the ridge and trotted along a goat path to an *alberca*, an irrigation pool, fed by rivulets from the mountains. He let the reins drop, permitting his horse to lap up the clear cold water. Turning in the saddle with a wince, he took in the view of his house below and its chapel adjacent to the village. The older he became, the closer he felt to this terrain, the more loath he was to make any further journeys away from it.

He patted the horse's strong neck, appreciating the warmth of it in the brisk air. Autumn, his favorite season, was imminent. He took a hank of the chestnut-hued mane in his elderly spotted hand, giving it an affectionate tug the horse ignored, but in doing so he awakened a memory he could have done without. An event connected with the dismal demise of the Armada twenty-four years earlier. All had been done to save the fleet. All hope of ferrying Parma's troops to France had been abandoned. He commanded his ships to flee north, trying to escape Drake's lighter vessels that persisted in attacking them like angry wasps from a bothered nest. It was September then, as well, but far colder when they rounded Scotland and came about, finally pointing south again. As they sailed along the western coast of Ireland, he tried to keep them well out at sea, but currents and storms that seemed to mock him drove the fleet landward. Many of the ships were damaged. Provisions and water supplies dwindled. Spirits were as foul as the weather. And then there came the moment when he had to order his cavalry officers to drive their mounts into the sea.

The sight of his sailors screaming aflame from the vile fire ships off of Gravelines, watching his cabin boy expire on deck from a musket wound, living with the ravaged faces of his troops ill with starvation and dysentery, none of these images affected him as much as seeing the horses being forced to dive into the cold sea, seeing their heads bobbing in the rough, deep, foreign waves as he left them behind to drown, so far from their paddocks in Andalusia.

At the midday meal that afternoon, Don Julian took the news of his being sent to the Medina-Sidonia palace in Sanlúcar with surprising pleasure. The Duke observed how Guada put on a brave smile. She thanked him for showing such confidence in her husband. But he would have sworn the girl was on the verge of tears.

– XI –

In which the Samurais reach Spain

Shiro stood by the bowsprit. The ship moved through the estuary. The shores on either side were gentle and uninhabited. The worst of the crossing was far behind them.

Sanlúcar de Barrameda in October smelled of whitewash, burning olive twigs, and tall dark sherry barrels rinsed with well water. The sun was clear and crisp, the land and the wide beaches flat against low green hills that beckoned in the distance. Immense white clouds slowly expanded and then dissipated in the breeze, propelling them while a pair of high-flying birds he could not identify soared among them.

Diego and all the Spaniards aboard were excitedly pointing to this and that from the deck and slapping one another's backs. Hasekura Tsunenaga appeared on deck wearing one of his better robes, one made from white silk with red cranes sewn into it. All of the Samurai wore black or navy with black lapels and sashes, their swords and scabbards polished for show.

As Shiro took in the landscape, he felt something he was not prepared for, a familiarity experienced as a trembling lightness within his chest. It was as if some spirit emanating from the land were speaking to him. How, he wondered, could a place so foreign and so unknown feel this way? He could not grasp it and thought at first it might be an effect common to those who travel great distances and spend long periods of time at sea. But the arrival at New Spain after crossing the Pacific, and the arrival in La Habana after crossing the Gulf of Mexico did not feel anything like this.

He noticed storks nesting atop the bell tower of a Christian church looming in the village ahead. They were birds—*Kounotori*—highly prized in his country. He bowed toward them and then made his way back to the helm to speak with Hasekura Tsunenaga and the Christian captain.

'May I have a word sir?'

The Japanese ambassador looked at him with some suspicion, for they had not exchanged a syllable since Shiro had been released from the hold months ago.

'You may.'

'I was wondering, with your permission and that of Señor Capitan Oquendo, if I might stand first watch aboard the ship once we've docked.'

Hasekura raised an eyebrow.

'Are you not as eager as everyone else to step upon the firmament?'

'I am sir, but I am just as glad to wait another day to do so.'

Once again the young man seemed to be angling for a special status. Hasekura Tsunenaga found it irritating.

'As you wish,' he said, though he continued to search his mind for some hidden motive. Shiro then repeated the request to the Spanish officer, who had no objection either, but who suggested Shiro present himself the following day to help translate when a representative of the King would arrive from Sevilla.

The reception at the quay was impeccable except for when Hasekura Tsunenaga tripped on the gangplank and almost lost his balance. Shiro counted fifteen coaches and carriages painted in bright pastel hues with gold edging and bedecked with plumes. The drivers wore pink and sky blue leggings and white powdered wigs. But the three young nobles on horseback did not dismount to receive Date Masamune's representative. The only deference they showed, clearly something they had discussed and agreed upon ahead of time, was to feign a brief bow from their saddles. Women carried parasols or wore veils and dressed in elaborate skirts and long-sleeved blouses with colorful *mantillas* on their heads held in place by sturdy combs made from tortoise shell and mother-of-pearl.

He was relieved when everyone had gone save for a small group of onlookers with nothing better to do than stare and make commentary about the new ship in port. As night fell, these too dispersed, and Shiro, content, walked the length and breadth of the decks as if he owned them. He served himself an extra ration of biscuits with his dried fish and an extra draft of water, and in the blackness afterwards he climbed all the way to the crow's nest, something he had been wanting to do since leaving Japan.

Holding on to the circular bannister stained with tern and gull droppings, he looked out upon the village. Many of the houses were dark and shuttered. Others were lit from within by tapers. Smoke wafted from chimneys, and up on a rise he imagined he saw the palace where the festivities were being held, for the lights were brightest in that part of the town, and it was from there that music could be heard that drifted across the rooftops. Turning about, there was nothing but darkness, dark currents running against a dark shore, a sandy strand being overrun by the swift night tide. Above, no moon, and a million stars.

He awakened two hours later, cramped and startled, cold and ashamed. Sleep was forbidden to the man on watch, and he could easily have fallen to a rude death. He raised his right hand in front of his face, contemplating the extra finger that, despite all that had been said since his birth, bothered him immensely.

He climbed back down to the deck and knelt by the helm, meditating in the cold, damp air, until dawn light appeared under a thin layer of clouds out by the low dunes and the curving shore. He stripped and lowered himself into the water on the far side of the ship and performed his ablutions and then swam in the cold water as the light increased. Back on board, he dried himself and dressed, just in time to meet the man sent to relieve him. Holding the hilt of his sword in the manner his Lord and uncle Date Masamune had taught him, he walked down the gangplank and for the first time felt the earth of Spain beneath his feet.

– XII –

In which a sword is broken and a vision beheld

Hasekura Tsunenaga preferred Father Sotelo as his principal translator. While Sotelo fawned before the King's representative and communicated pleasantry after pleasantry between Hasekura Tsunenaga and the heads of noble families, Shiro was left to mediate pointless conversations between merchants and local functionaries who were keen to mingle with the exotic Samurai. He soon realized that had he been a better nephew to his Lord, he would have made an effort during the long crossings to gain Hasekura Tsunenaga's confidence. Instead, he was being shunned and shut out.

After dinner Father Sotelo suggested that a gesture of gratitude be offered to the Duke of Medina-Sidonia for preparing such a festive reception in Sanlúcar. Hasekura Tsunenaga agreed and arranged for a gift and ordered Shiro to serve as the courier. Though Sotelo knew how powerful a man the Duke was, neither Hasekura Tsunenaga nor Shiro realized what an opportunity this mission of etiquette represented. Hasekura Tsunenaga was simply pleased to find a way to banish Shiro for a time, and in turn the young Samurai felt even more like an outcast. Diego volunteered to accompany him.

Before retiring that evening, they were told to visit Don Julian, the young Duke of Denia, in order to obtain a letter of presentation.

Thanks to his recent marriage, Julian occupied one of the better apartments on the upper floor of the palace overlooking the bay. When Shiro and Diego were shown in, Marta Vélez was in the sitting room holding a glass of wine. The young Duke appeared and introduced her as his aunt before leaving the three of them to write the letter. At first Marta Vélez was appalled at the idea of having to make conversation with such an odd duo. She ascribed it to the vicissitudes of life in the provinces. In Madrid a small army of servants, starting at the front door of her palacete and ending with her chambermaid, would have formed a wall of protection between such peculiar callers and her person. There in Sanlúcar, the three of them stood in excruciating silence listening to Julian scrawl his quill upon a sheet of parchment.

She could not deny that the young Samurai was handsome. He was tall and slender but with wide shoulders. He stood up straight and appeared relaxed, wrapped in a robe that was dark and elegant, standing upon a pair of noisy wooden sandals such as she had never seen. His companion however, with his stump and stained breeches and stringy long hair, looked to be the kind of man she spent her life avoiding. But he was Spanish, and it was to him she directed her first words.

'How is the foreigner finding our country?'

Diego looked down, waiting for Shiro to answer himself.

'I understand your language,' the Samurai said.

She looked at him.

'How extraordinary,' she said. 'You've hardly any accent.'

'And I am very pleased to be here,' he said. 'I am very pleased to be back on land.'

She seemed to find this funny and felt her spirits rising when she realized how this unexpected encounter would provide a delicious anecdote upon her return to Madrid. Diego then noticed that under her dress, she was barefoot.

'I know you have only been here a day,' she said to Shiro, 'but what do you most notice that is different for you?'

'Everything, madam,' he said. 'The food and how it is eaten, the manner of dress, the variety of faces and colors—the lack of baths.'

'Lack of baths.'

'Yes, madam. In Japan everyone bathes, and here I think not.'

'It is generally believed that water carries disease, entering through the pores of the skin, infecting us with plague.'

Shiro only smiled politely.

'You don't agree?' she asked him.

Again, he only smiled. She took note of how a Spaniard at this point would be raising his voice and counterarguing with baroque gesticulations. She smiled back at him.

'Well neither do I,' she said. 'And where I normally live, in Madrid, I have a room dedicated to bathing. If you come there someday, I shall show it to you.'

'This I would very much like to see,' he said.

It was unclear to all three of them whether there might or might not be some degree of flirtation in the air. Then Julian emerged and handed a sealed missive to Diego, ignoring Shiro completely.

'Here you go then.'

'Sir,' said Diego, somewhat slavishly, pleasing the young Duke.

Julian reached into a purse and pulled out three coins he then placed into Diego's hand that still held the letter. 'And this is for you if I can have your word no mention will be made of my aunt's presence here, a matter of some family tension you've no need to know about.'

'Not one word, sir,' Diego said, lowering his head.

Julian turned briefly to Shiro and bowed his head as he had to Hasekura Tsunenaga the day before. Then he left the room taking his aunt with him. But before Marta Vélez disappeared from view, she turned and gave Shiro a quick conspiratorial smile.

Once they were alone, she took her nephew's hand. 'That was rather rude,' she said.

'Not at all.'

'Well you might have given the foreigner some coins as well then because he speaks fluent Spanish.'

'No.'

'Yes.'

He paused and considered.

'But he won't say anything about us,' Julian said with a sneer. 'He'll be too busy running from the Duke's hounds.'

'I found him appealing.'

'That is because you are a loose woman of most unsound judgment. He's just a heathen, a freakish messenger in women's garb.'

***

Shiro and Diego left at dawn and reached Jerez in the afternoon, where they changed horses. By the time night was falling, they were still four hours from Medina-Sidonia. They made camp in a grove of pines next to a stream born off the Guadalete River. Shiro was tired of dried fish and cured meats and with his bow went out and downed three wood pigeons on the fly. Diego had never seen such a thing and talked about it ceaselessly while Shiro plucked and cleaned and roasted the birds. The ride thus far had been beautiful. Being on a horse again and hunting, resting like that in a forest by a fire, all of it was a blessing.

He regretted his friend's company. Diego had spoken too much since leaving Sanlúcar, going on about Phoenicians, Greeks, Romans, Moors, and Visigoths, all of the different peoples who had lived in those hills and valleys with the sea so close by. None of it really interested the Samurai, and all of it had interfered with the experience of simply being there. Diego was the sort, he realized, who had to speak, who required distraction from what, for Shiro, was the best part of being.

Early the next morning while the Spaniard slept, Shiro stripped and immersed himself in the stream. As the frigid water rushed over him, he decided there were advantages to being an outcast. Had his mother been married to his father, he would never have left Japan. The Lord would have recognized him, but only as he did the other heirs. Had he a real father, his spirit would have been overly molded. Being a bastard had set him free. Being a bastard had placed him there in that stream on the other side of the world. As one of his favorite monks always said to him whenever he complained of being slighted, 'Who knows what is good and what is bad?' This, it seemed, was one of the great divides between his Zen Confucianism and the beliefs espoused by the Christians, who professed to know in every instance what was correct and what was sinful.

When they arrived at the Duke's grand finca, he and Diego were told to wait at the gate. An hour passed before a secretary appeared to collect the letters. Two hours after that, the same man returned to say the letters had been read and that their presence was no longer necessary. Diego was angry for how it made his countrymen look, and angry at the nobility the way he had always been since youth, but he had no desire to quarrel with so powerful a house and prepared to remount his horse. Shiro remained calm and told the secretary he still had a gift to give the Duke and that he would only present it in person. He then added that in his own land he was considered a Prince and that if the Duke knew this, surely he would receive him.

When the secretary went away, Diego asked, 'Are you a prince?'

'My Lord Date Masamune has called me thus, for his blood runs through my veins.'

Diego nodded in admiration as if he understood, but the hierarchies and royal stations of the Japanese had never been clear to him. He thought to inquire further, but a steely gaze behind the young Samurai's aura of calm gave him pause. When the secretary returned, Shiro was admitted into the palace.

He admired the white walls and the dark wooden furniture and the tiled floors. The palace in Sanlúcar, though plain on the outside—someone had explained to him this feature derived from an Islamic ideal he found pleasing—was ornate and extravagant within. But here, where the owner felt most at home, the style was almost Japanese in that it was simple and austere within and without. Shiro liked the stark religious paintings and somber portraits, the austere suits of armor, the potted ferns and faded tapestries. It was the house of someone who felt no need to prove anything.

He was shown to the Duke's study, where the noble sat at a wide and heavy desk on which were piled papers and manuscripts. Putting down a magnifying glass and using his cane for support, he stood. Shiro bowed as the Duke studied the young man before him. In all of his travels and misadventures and with all of the foreign dignitaries he had met at court, never before had he seen anyone who looked like this.

'There is no mention of your royal status in either of the letters brought with you,' he said, speaking slowly for the other's benefit.

'And you've come accompanied by a man who looks like a stable hand.'

'I am Shiro-San, Prince of Sendai, my lord.'

The Duke smiled, impressed by the young man's pluck, and he took an immediate interest in the curious, long hilt of the oddly shaped sword protruding from Shiro's sash.

'In my country, this country, the term 'Prince' is reserved exclusively for legitimate heirs of the King, a King who rules all of Spain and Portugal, the Two Sicilies, the Low Countries, and all of New Spain and the Philippines across the ocean. What does it mean in your land?'

'There is no mention of my royalty in the letters I have brought with me because I am an illegitimate heir. The legitimate ones would never have traveled so far from their castles and armies. But I am related to and close to the Lord Date Masamune, who has sent me here to your country.'

The Duke was shocked and then amused by the young man's forthright admission and amused as well by the *sevillano* intonation with which he spoke.

'The man who wrote one of the letters, your countryman, is he a legitimate Prince?' asked the Duke.

'He is legitimate and of noble blood and has been entrusted by Lord Masamune to lead the Embassy mission, but he is not a prince.'

'And does he recognize you as such?'

'No, or rather, yes, which is why I suspect I am such a disturbance to him. He has sent me here with the letters to be rid of me.'

The Duke realized he was in the presence of a princely boy regardless of the details and was glad for the interruption. He motioned for Shiro to sit before returning to the chair at his desk.

'It tires me to stand.'

He tapped the tabletop with the unclipped nails of his right hand. 'Let me see if I understand what you are telling me,' he said. 'The King of your country who has sent the Embassy mission has chosen a member of the nobility to lead it. But you, even though you are illegitimate, and I will come to that in a minute, are closer to this King and thus resented by the noble ambassador.'

'Yes, my lord. That is an accurate assessment, except that the Lord Date Masamune would never refer to himself as a King.'

'And why is that?'

'He prefers to describe himself as a warrior.'

'Is he one?'

'Yes, sir.'

'And you?'

'I and my fellow Samurai, we are all warriors who follow the Warrior's Way. From what I have learned thus far, the Warrior's Way is similar to what here is called chivalry.'

'You don't much look like a warrior.'

'Why is that?'

'Warriors are rougher and tougher looking as a rule.'

'When one's sword is swift and sharp, there is no need for roughness. And a tough appearance is often deceptive.'

The Duke smiled.

'Is it true you have all been baptized? You and your fellow warriors?'

'Yes. All of us except for Hasekura Tsunenaga, who wishes to be baptized in the presence of your King.'

'And are you really believers in the tenets of the Church?'

'We are believers in diplomacy.'

The Duke laughed aloud. 'I am beginning to see why your ambassador might wish to keep you far away.'

Shiro did not react to this and instead remembered something.

'I bring you a gift from him.'

He reached into his tunic and took out a long dagger wrapped in soft leather. He stood and approached the desk and, bowing, presented it to the Duke, who took it from him.

'This is a treasured *Tanto*,' usually kept at one's side with the 'Katana,' he said touching the hilt of his sword. 'The combination of the two, and here is my own kept close to my heart, is known as the "*Daisho*." Only a Samurai may carry them.'

The Duke unwrapped the knife and took it in hand.

'It is very beautiful. It is a pleasing gift.'

'And sharp.'

'I am most honored.'

'The honor is mine, sir. You have received us, after our long journey, far better than we once received your sailors who, blown off course, came to our shores. We have much to learn from you in this regard.'

The Duke thought for a moment about his son and his daughter-in-law, and then focused on the odd young man come to his study in the hills from a land he would never visit, and he felt the weight of his years.

'I suggest you make no great haste to be pleased with us just yet, sir. Do you know why I did not receive you right away this morning?'

'No.'

'Because of the second letter, written by my countryman, the husband in fact of my very own niece. Shall I read it to you?'

Shiro simply nodded his head.

'I shall skip the flowery salutations that, between you and me, should have told me all I needed to know about this boy, and proceed to the pith of the matter.'

He cleared his throat and then held the letter in both his hands up close to his watery eyes.

'Rather than taking the effort to come himself, the ambassador has entrusted his greetings and message of gratitude to, from what I can deduce, the lowest of the low, the young man who was ordered to stay on board their ship as a guard last night along with some common sailor from La Triana who can barely read. The insult, or worse, the ignorance thus revealed, astonishes me. Needless to say, you must not even acknowledge their presence when and if they arrive.'

He placed the letter back down upon the desk.

'What do you make of that?'

Listening to the contents of the letter, Shiro decided to make the author pay for his slander, but he kept it to himself.

'When Hasekura Tsunenaga came off the ship,' he said to the Duke in a tone of equanimity, 'neither Don Julian nor his two comrades deigned to dismount their horses to meet our ambassador face-to-face. Then the other evening, when my friend and I went to obtain from him this letter of presentation, he did not speak a word to me but only addressed my friend Diego, to whom he gave some money in exchange for silence regarding a certain woman who was there with him. And I was never ordered to stay aboard the ship. I volunteered to do so.'

The Duke raised his eyebrows with true fascination. What had started out as an ordinary morning dulled by paperwork and the tedium of old age was redeemed.

'A woman, you say.'

'A woman he called his aunt but who clearly was not.'

This was not a topic of great interest to the Duke.

'And who is this Diego fellow everyone thinks so little of?'

'He is from Sevilla, an adventurer. A fine man.'

'But why is he with you?'

'We became friends during the journey from Japan, making fun of Father Sotelo. And then I saved his life. So he is grateful.'

'Father Sotelo.'

'The Spanish priest who taught me your language in Japan, also from Sevilla, and the man behind our entire mission, for I believe it was his idea that the Lord agreed to.'

'And how did you come to save the sailor's life?'

'He made the mistake of drawing a knife on a Samurai, who then sliced off his hand and was about to behead him when I intervened.'

'Behead the man, you say, on the deck of the ship?'

'Beheading is a common practice, where it takes place is secondary. As it was, the Samurai performed *seppuku* in front of everyone.'

'Which is?'

'We open the abdomen with the tanto, like the one you have now. It is a sign of respect for one's adversary.'

'Good lord. How revolting.'

'No more so than when one hunts and then guts an antelope.'

'Speaking of innards, mine are getting stirred. We must eat something. But I have just one more question. Why did you volunteer to stand guard on the ship? Why would a Prince, even an illegitimate one, wish to do such a thing?'

'We had come so far sir, so far from where I am from, from who I am, and suddenly, entering the channel at Sanlúcar de Barrameda, I felt too strangely at home, and such was my state of consternation I needed time alone before stepping ashore. Being alone, after so many months of forced comradeship, was the great luxury. In truth, I only conceded to have Diego accompany me here to your house because he wished to. The idea of being alone in your countryside with a horse and my bow was what I wanted.'

Down in the garden next to the chapel, the two men took Málaga wine and a selection of pastries made by nuns cloistered in the village convent. Pomegranates and mottled quince hung from trees, late roses flourished, low-clipped hedges of acrid-smelling boxwood neatened the perimeters. Though a pallet of greens predominated, fallen leaves decorated the gravel paths and a telltale autumn damp competed with the sunlight.

The Duke held Shiro's Katana in both his bony hands, noting its balance, shape and craftsmanship. Shiro held a Spanish fencing sword that had been brought with the refreshments.

'I am a strong defender of what we call *La Verdadera Destreza*,' said the Duke, 'the true art of swordsmanship, as opposed to the *esgrima vulgar*. I've paid for a book to be published on the topic, and among our nobility there is much lively discussion between the *Carrancistas* and the *Pachequistas* with regard to what constitutes proper footwork and such. But as you can see, we only employ one hand. Do you think you might give me a short demonstration of how it is you Samurai wield your swords?'

One of the guards was summoned, and in a small clearing by a fountain Shiro and the man squared off. Shiro bowed to the guard before assuming his first position, and this impressed the Duke. But nothing could have prepared him for what came next, the acrobatics of the Samurai sword swirling above Shiro's head, behind him, and then dramatically surging forward at a precise angle with respect to Shiro's elbows. The guard did his best to represent the Duke's enthusiasm for the *verdadera destreza,* but within half a minute, enough time in which to show his host some of the basic moves, Shiro went at his opponent's sword and cut it in half, breaking through its blade as if the barbarian steel were a dried twig.

The severed blade flew up into the limpid air, shimmering in the sun. The three men followed it with their eyes. It went the length of the garden, spinning between oleander blossoms and palm fronds. Missing her delicate foot by less than an inch, it finally came to rest sticking firmly into the earthen path where Guada tred, her head covered and her heart contrite after mass in the chapel.

– PART TWO –

PART TWO

– XIII –

In which Shiro and Guada walk among the ruins

In a corner of the large room assigned to him, a taper projected tentacles of amber light upon the whitewashed wall. The bed was broad and hard. Shiro lay beneath a sheet of bleached muslin graced with a band of embroidery stitched along the top that intertwined the Duke's initials with astrological themes. Over the sheet was draped a heavy coverlet made from the skins of lynxes hunted in the Sierra of Grazalema. It was finished with a border of frayed burgundy velvet. The coverlet's warmth compensated for the gelid air entering through the open shutters, air that carried scents of pine and rosemary.

His head ached. It was just before dawn, and he listened to the clip-clop and occasional slipping of mule hooves navigating the rocky surface of a nearby street. He imagined it was being lead out of the village into the countryside. Though he felt far from home, once again there was something familiar here.

He thought about the wondrous girl. At supper the previous evening, he would have sworn her eyes rose at the ends into a slight slant. The elegance of her bearing, the subtlety of her, had overwhelmed him. When he caught her staring at the extra finger on his right hand, an extravagance the Duke had yet to notice, it tied his tongue.

The thought she was married to the rude barbarian, the one called Julian who had paid Diego not to mention the woman they found him with in Sanlúcar, was puzzling. At first he assumed the marriage had been arranged, but each time Julian's name arose in conversation, she reacted favorably. He could see she cared for her husband, and it had taken all the control he could muster to stifle an urge to reveal what he knew.

It was not hard for him to imagine that had he been able to spend more time with Yokiko, love might have followed, love for a girl enslaved to other men. He'd been told his own mother had passionately loved her first husband, a handsome Samurai not known for his kindness, but then she'd found love again with Katakura Kojuro, a rotund and ungainly sort married to someone else.

He knew he would have to resign himself to the fact that even if Guada had not already been claimed, anything beyond the exchange of pleasantries would be impossible. Neither her tribe of privileged Christians nor his Samurai code would sanction anything but a most politic and constrained friendship. It was in fact her condition as a married woman—and his as an exotic foreign guest—that permitted them a measure of freedom. Had she been unattached, she would never have been unaccompanied, even under the protection of her uncle's vaulted ceilings. As it was, her mother was due to arrive in a few days' time to "relieve" the Duke from having to devote so large a fraction of his diminishing energies toward the entertainment of his niece.

Bits of goat braised over a fire had been served with potatoes grown from plantings brought from the New World. The meat was garnished as well with apples and pears. The wine, something he had never tasted, came from the north of Spain, something the Duke seemed quite pleased about. As he kept drinking it, he found his tongue loosened, and it was the discussion about *maguro* that finally provoked Shiro to shake his shyness altogether. A small village along the coast nearby within the Duke's domain was known for its families of vigorous tuna fishermen. When the Duke mentioned how the season had begun, Shiro told them what a great a delicacy the fish was in the land he came from. The Duke then insisted they make the excursion that would get underway that morning within the next few hours.

By noon, from high in the hills they spied the sea. With the Duke, Shiro, Guada, and Rosario, and then the Duke's guards and servants, it was a colorful caravan that wound its way through the green grasses of the gentle slopes and their almond trees. The Duke was dressed in cream and crimson, Shiro in black and white, Guada mounted sidesaddle wearing a billowing ivory-hued skirt and a waistcoat of teal blue with yellow buttons fashioned from Venetian glass. Rosario wore black. The guards wore gray and blue, the servants, muslin tunics. The chaplain had been left behind. One guard riding ahead carried the Duke's standard fastened to a long, varnished pole. A string of pack mules carrying tents and provisions trailed behind.

In all his life thus far, Shiro had never known terrain like this. Autumn felt like spring. Everything shimmered under a sun that warmed the skin without oppressing. It was a land unblemished by husbandry, interrupted only sparingly by an occasional white house, always with two windows and a tiled roof and sustained by a modest patch of vegetables and a simple sty of small gray pigs. Nothing malign intruded.

For the Duke it was different. Each step taken by his stallion sent stabbing pains through the proud man's hip. That morning's flagon of wine had done little to dull it. But his vanity, his masculinity, his desire to remain, if only in his own mind, a romantic figure for Rosario, to remain connected by a solid line to a youthful past in which he'd been an envied roué at court kept him going in stoic denial of how little time his body would allow him to stand erect unaided.

They reached the shore by late afternoon, where a steady wind from the straits blew beige clouds of sand at their ankles. After consulting with local fishermen, they unloaded the mules behind low dunes near a pond at the edge of a sizeable extension of Roman ruins. Numerous tall columns and the remains of an amphitheater and streets leading nowhere paved with blocks of neatly placed stones imbued the encampment with an air of antiquity. Shiro implored upon the Duke immediately.

'What place is this?'

'I am pained to say I know very little. Some years back I paid two scholars a handsome sum to explore it, but their findings were scant. They thought it had once been called Baelo Claudia, for the Emperor Claudius had given it the status of a municipium in the First Century. It was a town devoted to fishing and to the production of garum and had once boasted temples dedicated to Isis, Jupiter, and Minerva.'

Shiro knew little about the Romans or their emperors, and the Duke was cajoled to impart a history lesson on the spot that all within earshot took pleasure from. He aptly brought his lecture to an end with references to some of his ancestors who had helped recover the territory from Moorish rule in the middle of the 13th century.

That night they ate ribs of pork and sipped a wine diluted with water. Soon after the Duke retired, Rosario was summoned to his tent.

Shiro invited Guada on a stroll about the ruins, lit that night by a new moon. A guard followed them maintaining a discrete distance.

A damp chill was in the air. It seemed to rise from the cracks between the millennial stones they walked upon. Holding her cloak tight about her neck, Guada realized she had never strolled at night, at anytime really, unaccompanied, with a man not her husband, and what an unusual man this one was.

'Once upon a time this was an active town on the sea,' she said, 'filled with men, women, and children living under the protection of Roman law, and all the time they lived here, they assumed it would go on forever. Now no one remembers them.'

She knew how banal it sounded, even as the words left her lips, but she also felt it was up to her to initiate conversation with the stranger who, the evening before, had spoken so little.

'Impermanence is a condition of life,' he said. 'These ruins are good reminders. We have places like this in my country.'

She knew nothing about his country, had only learned of its existence the other day, and her sense of geography was elementary at best.

'I don't think I like the way that sounds,' she said, 'about impermanence.'

'Why?'

'It frightens me,' she said. 'I like who and how and where I am now. I don't like for things to change.'

'But you know they will.'

'Of course,' she said. 'I know some day I will grow old and die, as surely as we are here tonight. But I don't like it.'

'I don't like it either,' he said. 'But I think it can be helpful for— how to live each day.'

'It sounds like it might be sinful.'

'How?'

'Like it might lead to temptation.'

'Your religion is very concerned with temptation.'

'It is your religion, too.'

He decided not to challenge her on this point.

'And the idea,' he said, 'that one is always being watched from on high, and judged, and that one will be tried after one's death is very, how shall I put it. . .'

'Tiring?'

He laughed. They both laughed.

'Yes,' he said. 'Just the word.'

'But we are born to struggle,' she said, 'to struggle against sin, just as animals struggle to survive. Relinquishing our vigilance is unbecoming to God.'

They paused and rested upon an uneven ledge of stone, the remnant of a wall that faced the sea. The sea was only visible at that hour because of the moon.

'These people who lived here so long ago,' he said, 'these Romans, were they Christians, do you think?'

'I doubt it. The Duke mentioned temples built for mythic deities, but none dedicated to the Savior.'

'They too struggled,' he said, 'to survive, as you say. But how, according to our religion, would they have been judged after death?'

'They would have been, all of them, condemned to hell for eternity.'

'Does that seem fair?' he asked.

'It is best not to question these issues. It, too, can lead to sin.'

'In some of our mountain villages, when the elderly are no longer useful, they are carried off to a place and left to die.'

'That is unfair.'

'I agree. But I fail to see any difference.'

'Those who are not members of the Church worship false gods by definition, and that is a sin, a mortal sin.'

'How lucky I am,' he said, 'to have been saved.'

She looked at him.

'Are you toying with me?'

'A little,' he said. 'Is that, too, a sin?'

'I shall pray for you,' she said, 'to St. Thomas perhaps, for your doubting soul, and to St. Joseph, who is the patron of a happy death, because when he died, Jesus and Mary were at his side.'

'You are too kind,' he said.

She knew he was mocking her, but she did not mind. She had never had a conversation like this before.

'I'm cold,' she said. 'Let us return to the camp.'

He stood and helped her off the ledge, touching her hands for the first time. He wanted to kiss her, and she knew it.

They began to walk back. The guard bowed as they went past him, a bow Shiro acknowledged with one of his own. They returned in silence, one that made sleep difficult for the both of them. Once in his tent, Shiro listened to the waves and the wind while picturing the coast of Edo so far away in what felt like another lifetime. Guada clung fiercely to a pair of gloves given to her by Julian, smelling them, resting her head upon them, missing her husband with an intensity that bordered on anger.

– XIV –

In which a night wind blows and confidences are exchanged

Rosario and the Duke lay under a coverlet listening to the wind buffeting the tent. Of all the young women over the years with whom he had exercised his *droit de seigneur*, she was, by far, his favorite. Her beauty, her seeming obliviousness to his age, her openness to pleasure, the offhand way she took his money, the clarity she maintained between what they did together and the rest of her life.

'How are things with your husband?' he asked.

'Difficult,' she said. 'He keeps trying to get me pregnant.'

He wondered if she said it to irk him, which it did.

'It's time for that, I suppose. And he must, of course, desire you fiercely.'

'I do not feel his desire. He only wants a child so that our families will stop making fun of him.'

'To expect anything else from a man like that is foolish.'

'That is what my mother says.'

'She was always wise.'

She kissed his bare shoulder. He closed his eyes to savor it.

'What was she like—then?' she asked.

'Quiet, angry at first. But that changed over time.'

'Are you certain I am not your daughter?'

'She assured me you weren't.'

'What if she is wrong?'

'I think women know such things. If you became pregnant by me, wouldn't you know who the father was?'

'That would be easy. Antonio is short and hairy. You are tall and handsome.'

'Bless you. But I am an old man.'

'Not with me,' she said. 'I should never have married him.'

'If you hadn't, you would have been forced into a convent. Seeing you like this under those circumstances would have been much more difficult.'

For however sinful a thought, part of her wished he was her father. Her own had been coarse and mean. Then she imagined herself in the convent back up in the village, where the nuns were only glimpsed at mass through a Moorish grill when they sang hymns. Or you could only see their hands when they placed the pastels they made through the small iron bars in exchange for coins.

'Have you ever been with a nun?'

'Once.'

'What was she like?'

'Hairy, like your husband.'

They laughed aloud together.

'What do you make of our guest,' he asked her, 'the stranger from the Orient?'

'I have never seen anything like him. I wonder if he might be a devil.'

'But he is handsome.'

'Yes.'

'Do you think Guada likes him?'

'Guada is too in love with her *esposo* to notice anyone else.'

'How do you know?'

'She's told me. She has said it often since arriving here.'

'Too often perhaps.'

'You are an evil man, Your Excellency.'

'I care about her happiness. Is that so evil?'

'But she is already happy.'

'That's what she tells herself and the world. But her husband is a bit of a scoundrel, more than she knows.'

'Woman can be in love with scoundrels.'

She sat up. The whiteness of her slender back and the blackness of her hair caught him by surprise. She began to put her long tresses up with pins.

'And you think there may be something between them?' she asked.

'Have you not noticed?'

'My mind has been too occupied with you.'

He kissed a small dimple near the base of her spine.

'You are an evil girl.'

'I have been an evil girl, but now I must be a good girl again and return to Guada's tent.'

– XV –

In which sushi is served and a hand is asked for

Shiro woke and swam at dawn. No one entered the sea willingly at any time of the year there, and the local fishermen who saw him thought him mad. The water was cold and clear, but once accustomed to it he felt a surge of invigoration that approached a state of grace. Looking back to shore, he took in the wide sweeping beach, the towering dune at its western edge, the ruins of Baelo Claudia, the tops of the Duke's encampment where the Gúzman colors fluttered in the steady wind.

By the time the others appeared, Shiro had befriended the tuna fishermen and a roundup was under way. Skiffs placed a wide net out from the shore held by buoys that horses on the sand drew slowly shoreward. As the muscular school of bluefin tuna, massive and silvery, began to understand what was happening, they started to panic and thrash, turning the diminishing volume of water into a spectacle of frothing foam. Awaiting them on the beach was a group of executioners clad in rags, armed with hooks and spikes. Off to the side, the Duke and his retinue observed the proceedings. The men waded into the low breaking waves, meting out mighty blows that turned the water crimson. Shiro, wearing little more than a loincloth, walked among the dying victims looking for the best specimen. Though focused on the task at hand, he could not help but remember the careless slaughter of the elephant seals he'd witnessed on the beach in San Simeon.

The two young women, plus some of the guards and locals, found it hard to look away from Shiro's lean body, tall and taut, gleaming with blood and salt water. Guada finally did avert her gaze when instinct cautioned that sin was near. Soon after the last fish was hauled to shore, the young Samurai chose one that a guard then promptly paid for. Using his *tanto,* Shiro gutted it on the spot. The rapidity of the cuts and the knowledge it displayed impressed the tuna men, and the Duke enjoyed it, knowing it would somehow raise his reputation in their eyes.

At the midday meal, served about a makeshift table, Shiro presented them with small slices of *toro* carefully sliced from the bluefin's underbelly. They were bite-sized and gleaming, pressed upon small clusters of Calasparra rice harvested from the low mountains of Murcia. The Duke, Rosario, and the Duke's chef were the only ones willing to try it. Guada found it difficult to look at and regarded the presentation as yet another example of the young man's primitivism. She used this latest affront to her sensibility in conjunction with the sacrilegious tone he used in his conversation during their walk the night before, the ignorance of modesty displayed by his casual nakedness in the sea, the manner in which he swam and waded through the bloodied water, his eyes, the hair pulled back into a short tail, the odd clothing and armament, to reinforce her opinion as to his extreme and troublesome foreignness. She found her uncle's fascination with his guest disconcerting and was disappointed when she realized that Rosario, whom she had come to like and confide in, was having some sort of relationship with the Duke, a idea she felt to be obscene and tasteless. Were it up to Guada, they would return to Medina-Sidonia that very day. But her uncle was insisting upon another night by the unsettling ruins and the infernal waves that she now believed carried all manner of harmful humors within their ceaseless, wind-sprayed emanations. For reasons she could not, or simply would not, try to uncover, she'd been uncomfortable within her own skin since waking that day. She was even looking forward to her mother's visit, willing to trade the restrictions Doña Inmaculada's presence would impose, to regain some sense of normalcy. Why had Julian left her side so eagerly?

That afternoon Shiro disappeared into the hills to practice his physical and spiritual 'regimen.' But when, upon his return, he invited Guada to accompany him once again on a walk, this time by the sea, she turned him down. Stifling a sensual tremor the invitation provoked, she rechanneled it into a sensation of discomfort she ascribed to an indisposition she blamed on prolonged exposure to the maritime climate. He of course, as she expected, expressed surprise.

'Where I come from, the sea and its surroundings are among the most salutary to be found.'

'Nevertheless,' she said, but she had nothing else with which to further her assertion. After allowing her voice to trail off, she added, as if to bolster the wall between them, 'It is yet another example, I suppose, of the differences between us.'

Shiro took his walk alone while the Duke slept a long siesta. Rosario was vexed from having to pray a long novena on her knees next to Guada in their tent. The rote succession of Ave Marias spoken to the sandy floor made her sleepy, and it was only her fear of being reprimanded by the all-too-virtuous young lady beside her that kept her rigidly in place.

But with the arrival of night, she was able to relax, even though it seemed the darkness only increased the tension radiating from

Guada. Rosario ate the evening meal with gusto, as did the Duke, the foreigner, and everyone else with the exception of Guada. Afterwards it took all the patience Rosario had to wait for Guada to fall asleep so that she could go to the Duke once again. And when she rose to leave, convinced the blonde beauty was finally wrapped in slumber, Guada spoke out.

'What is it, Rosario?'

'Ma'am?'

'Where are you going at such an hour?'

'To relieve myself ma'am.' It was a statement not altogether untrue.

'Go then, but do not tarry. It is not safe out there.'

'We are surrounded by armed guards, ma'am.'

Frustrated, she entered the Duke's tent and reported his niece's sleeplessness.

'Let her be,' he said.

'My Lord?'

'Stay here with me.'

'But she will surely come looking for me if I do not return.'

'I doubt it. And if she does, so be it then.'

She remained standing, trying to understand what felt different in the air.

'But if she were to say anything,' she said, 'back at the finca—my reputation . . .'

'What would you say if I asked you to marry me, Rosario?'

The winds were unusually strong that night, and the leather flap at the entrance to the tent made a jarring noise at odds with the stillness within. Next to the wavering taper, the Duke had lit a stick of pomegranate incense that filled the air with a scent she would always identify with him. She came in farther.

'I am already married, my Lord.'

'To an individual I do not wish for you to ever return to.'

The statement, uttered with quiet simplicity, shocked her.

'I am getting on,' he said, 'and you are a young woman. But we are good together. Would you not agree?'

She smiled. 'I would, my Lord.'

'Spending time away from you no longer amuses me. Solitude, which has served me well this past decade, no longer amuses me. Having to conduct my personal life in secrecy as if I were a criminal or an adolescent does not become me. I find I have a deep affection for you. So would you have me, a gray man who has trouble walking?'

'I do not know what to say, my Lord.'

'A simple yes will do,' he said gently.

'If I could, my Lord, nothing would please me more.'

'Do you mean that? Tell me the truth.'

She fell to her knees before him, took his hand, kissed it, and then, still clinging to it, rested her head upon it. It was a narrow hand, but strong in sinew, and the thick gold of the ring on his middle finger was cold and wondrous pushing against her cheek.

'I mean it from the bottom of my heart,' she said.

And it was true because her heart was racing.

'Then I shall have your marriage annulled,' he said, 'on the grounds of your husband's infertility. The Pope is an old friend, and I'm sure Antonio's honor can be assuaged by a chest of coins emblazoned with the King's likeness.'

'A union with me would attract scandal to your reputation. I have no royal blood, my Lord.'

'I am the Admiral of the High Seas, a Grandee of Spain. I can do as I wish. And as for your lack of "royal blood" as you call it, my own ancestors, without rummaging too far back, were surely sheep herders or *oliveros* with blood like yours running through their veins. Our children shall have our blood combined.'

She did not return to Guada. Though incensed by the girl's boldness and by the fact she had been lied to, Guada was too embarrassed to protest. For the guards to observe her storming into her uncle's tent for the purpose of punishing the girl would be unsightly and unforgiveable. What she found herself thinking about instead was how close the Samurai's tent was to hers. Was he asleep, or awake like she? As she lay there, she was gripped by a fantasy difficult to control in which sticking her arm out from under her tent, feeling the narrow path of cold sand between them, she slipped her hand into his tent and gently placed her fingers upon his bare shoulder.

– XVI –

In which a Christian loses his head

On the next day, heavy clouds settled above that part of the coast. As the Duke and his retinue decamped and began their journey back up into the low mountains, a steady drizzle of autumn rain fell. Invigorated by the recklessness of his proposal and by having it accepted, and enjoying the sensation of keeping it secret for another day or two, the Duke barely noticed the weather or the pain in his hip. Rosario, too, still in shock, rode along side of Guada, stunned, exhilarated, fearful, but also serene, enjoying a degree of self-confidence new to her. Shiro took pleasure casting furtive glances at Guada while savoring the smells rising from the earth and shrubs. The guards and the cooking staff were bedraggled and tired.

One of them, a soldier called Guillermo, who had been in the Duke's service for many years, permitted himself to wallow in a sullen state of mind. He had a friend in the village close to Rosario's husband, and he had seen the girl entering the Duke's tent. Assuming his Lord had done nothing more than exercise his feudal rights, the soldier felt only scorn for the girl and looked forward to ruining her reputation upon their return. Bored and emboldened, he spurred his mount and rode up next to her.

'Who shall you confess to first, señora, to the priest or your husband?'

She looked at him, wide-eyed.

Not entirely meaning to, it had escaped his lips more loudly than he intended, loud enough for Guada to hear it word for word.

Up until that moment, Guada had been angry with Rosario; for the lie, for her behavior, for the girl's decision to not even ask forgiveness for last night's scandalous absence, the degree of self-assurance with which she had greeted Guada earlier that day. But the guard's tone was so foul and offensive, it disturbed her more, not to mention the fact he had taken the liberty of proclaiming his insult, for however just it might be, so close to her person. Just as she was on the verge of saying something, the man compounded his offense tenfold.

'If you wish to avoid a public beating,' he said to Rosario, this time lowering his voice, 'you'd best come round to my pallet on your way home tonight.'

Rosario reached across and slapped his unshaven face. Despite the rain and the hooves splashing in the mud, the retort was heard by all, and the Duke, interrupting his conversation with Shiro, turned in his saddle in time to see Guillermo grab Rosario by the wrist, twisting it, causing her to cry out. He called the caravan to a halt.

Overconfident that his status as a trusted guard would trump any influence a village girl might have, Guillermo now raised his voice for all to hear. 'Proof if I ever saw it of what the village says about you, girl . . .'

The Duke walked his stallion in between the horses Guillermo and Rosario sat upon, pushing them apart.

'Pray tell sir, what might that be?'

'Your Excellency?'

'I wish to hear it.'

'That she is not a Christian, my Lord, but a Jew, or even an Infidel.'

'Which, in your opinion, would be the worse of the two?'

'The Moors are our sworn enemies, my Lord.'

'And what is this all about? What has occurred here? What was the provocation that caused her to strike you?'

It was not a question the soldier wished to answer. He looked down at the muddy earth and then out at a green hill covered with bare almond trees.

'Guillermo?'

Guada, seizing upon the chance to voice her own bottled-up suspicions, answered instead.

'He accused her of indecent behavior, and . . .' but she could not bring herself to finish.

'And?'

Everyone could see the anger rising through the veins of the Duke's face.

'That if I knew what was good for me,' Rosario said, staring at the mane of her chestnut mare, at the wet, glistening leather of the reins in her small hands, 'I should come to him in the night, or else he would assure my humiliation.'

'Up until this moment,' said the Duke, looking at the soldier, 'the weather notwithstanding; this has been a glorious day for me. Could you guess why, Guillermo?'

'No sir.'

'Because last night I asked this woman you have just insulted, insulted in a most grievous and unforgiveable fashion, for her hand, and she graced me with her approval.'

93

This caught everyone's attention. The following silence was such that the rain sounded thunderous. As the irretrievable nature of his error wound its way about his gut, all Guillermo could bring himself to say was, 'My Lord.'

'And so now, I must ask for your hand,' said the Duke. 'Get down from your horse.'

Both men dismounted. The Duke drew his sword.

'Down on the ground, man, and out with your arm.'

'Please, sir.'

'What were you thinking? Even if I had never made this young woman's acquaintance, what sort of ruffian are you, what sort of Christian? Down in the mud with you.'

'But she's already married sir,' Guillermo blurted out, wide-eyed with fear, but with rage, as well, spittle surging forth through the rain, giving voice to a thought that all who were present had.

The Duke turned and faced the rest of his guards. 'I am loath to ask this of you, but it seems I must. Grab him and hold him down.'

The men dismounted, following the order with little hesitation. Whatever solidarity they felt with their comrade was overshadowed by relief it was someone else suffering the Duke's wrath. Then Guillermo drew his sword.

'I'll tell you what sort of Christian I am,' he said, yelling out for all to hear, 'the sort who follows the commandments and condemns adultery.'

Both Guada and Rosario were horrified to see the Duke raise his sword in turn, preparing to do battle with the renegade. The other soldiers stood their ground, hands upon their hilts.

'Stand back,' said the Duke. 'I swear by Almighty God that if I go down at the hand of this man, he'll go down with me. Let us see what you are made of.'

'My Lord—please,' said Rosario.

Guada shot a glance of alarm at Shiro, a glance that above all was an entreaty, a glance that contained all manner of emotions he grasped at once. He dismounted quickly and strode into the circle that had been formed around the two combatants.

'May I speak, my Lord,' he said to the Duke.

'If you must,' the Duke replied, not taking his eye off Guillermo.

'I offer you my services. It is unseemly for a noble of your station to have to deal with a man of such a rank. To ask for one of his own to deal with him, though a more just alternative, would be difficult for them, for they have fought alongside him. I beg of you to allow me, as your guest, to do what I am trained to, I who am only passing through here, I who would be grateful for the opportunity to repay, in some small measure, your hospitality.'

'The offense was committed against me, my friend. It is for me to address.'

'I've no doubt that address it you surely can. I only ask this of you as a favor to me.'

The Duke was about to refuse him again when Guillermo, a massive man, spoke up yet again, sealing his fate definitively.

'I'll take on the two of you. If you'd been my guest,' he said, looking at Shiro, 'I'd have had you in a cage by now to show the village children for their amusement.'

The Duke looked at Shiro. 'Very well, then.'

Rosario and Guada made the sign of the cross in thanks for this change of heart. Though the Duke did not yet place his sword back in its scabbard, he stood back, taking the reins of Rosario's horse to hold it steady.

'Give them room,' he said to the men.

Everyone moved back. The chef's assistants had to force their mules off the road into a small pasture. Shiro drew his sword and focused on what would be his second opportunity for real combat, his first with an authentic barbarian. The brutish guard, with little to lose, lunged at him forthwith, hoping to catch the slender foreigner unprepared, but Shiro stepped back and let the man fly past him, the long, heavy Christian blade piercing nothing but rain. Shiro stood his ground and allowed Guillermo time enough to turn around and catch his breath.

'You'll not escape me for very long,' barked the Spaniard.

It was then that Shiro sliced the man's sword hand off. It was done before anyone could really see it, in a single motion that was followed by another, a deep cut into the man's abdomen that brought the guard to his knees. Shiro spun, fixed his mark, and then relieved Guillermo of his head. He would later tell others and try and tell himself he performed this coup de grâce as an act of mercy, to save the man from the pain and humiliation about to invade him from the loss of his hand and the stench of his loosening guts, and he would reiterate, to the Duke later in the day as the soggy group approached the outskirts of Medina-Sidonia, that decapitation was the norm for warriors convicted of treason against their Lord. But inside, he knew he had done it out of hubris, letting those within the

Duke's employ who had pegged him for a freakish fop to see whom they were dealing with.

Many of the younger guards had yet to see battle. For the older men, those who had served with Guillermo and the Duke aboard the Armada, scenes like this had all but slipped from memory. In seconds their compatriot had gone from being a fearsome, angry man to a bloody trunk of meat. The chef, his workers, and the rest of the servants had recoiled in shock.

Rosario reacted to the spectacle with deep sobs the Duke did his best to assuage. And Guada, rigid in her saddle and pale as chalk, stared at the severed hand and its sword so as to avoid contemplating the ghoulish remains of the man or the blood-splattered figure of Shiro. She felt responsible. She had asked for his intervention with her eyes. The Samurai she had decided to disdain so recently had answered her call and probably saved her uncle's life. All of this she attempted to process within the mad beating of her heart along with the scandalous declaration the Duke had made with respect to her handmaiden and the base excitement Shiro's savage execution stirred within her. She bound it all together and hated her husband for having left her to deal with all of this alone, and she prayed for the day they might be united again in Sevilla.

As his blade passed through the Christian's neck and vertebra, Shiro had taken hold of the fact that he was ending a man's life. It was a life that had started decades earlier, born to a woman who had surely cooed and swaddled her newborn and who had taught the boy to walk and talk. The boy had grown into a man and had traveled and seen much and had staked out a manner in which to regard himself and survive. The man had wakened that day by the sea with his mind intact, filled with a confusion of memories and sensations and pedestrian concerns without giving the merest thought to when his death might arrive, blissfully unaware that only hours remained to him. The lesson was there, one Date Masamune had spoken to him about before Shiro took leave of Sendai Castle. 'Each sunrise,' the Lord had said, 'each breath you take, brings you closer to death. Breathe deeply and be where you are.'

– XVII –

In which youth is scorned

Marta Vélez tired of her nephew. Julian's conversation was limited to little more than opportunities to speak well of himself. She had stayed too long in Sanlúcar. The damp sea air drained her and made her hair unruly. She longed for the mountainous, dry climate of Madrid. She missed her own house and servants. She missed the lazy grandeur of court with its fierce rivalries cloaked in faux religiosity.

Waiting for Julian to return each afternoon, invariably drunk after frittering away the morning hours with rich and rancid provincial friends who never seemed to tire of the same stories told in one of two taverns, had become unbearable. The only thing keeping her there was the discomfort and angst she felt at being alone. But after last night's debilitating argument, she was ready to go. Once back in Madrid, she would renew her dinner parties and be kinder to Don Rodrigo during his visits to court. Perhaps a new admirer might be found less related to her by blood and more interesting to share her bed with.

Feigning sleep until Julian left one morning to find his friends, she made haste with her toilette, ordering a servant to pack and hire a carriage. When he returned for the midday meal holding a large bouquet of mimosa, he hoped her ill humor might have passed, that he might get her to laugh and undress for him again. A comely young serving girl he and his mates had bantered with earlier in the day had put him in the mood for a *siesta amorosa*.

But after slapping the servant for obeying Marta's commands and ransacking their suite of rooms in fruitless search for a note of explanation, throwing the sprigs of mimosa to the floor, he collapsed in a corner and cried. As a small boy, his mother left him often when she would go to be with his father in distant castles and provinces, abandoning him to fend for himself. She would go off without a second thought, eager to give her body to his revolting sire.

Marta's departure coincided with the only event Julian truly had to attend that very afternoon, as the Duke of Medina-Sidonia's personal emissary. Since the arrival of the Japanese Delegation, he had largely ignored his official obligations. He had taken it upon himself to decide that the Duke's attitude toward the foreigners should be one of condescension. Wrapped in a flag of aristocratic snobbery, he'd been able to justify his inclination to avoid almost every opportunity for improving relations with the Japanese, while giving ample rein to his debaucheries. It did not go unnoticed by local officials with ties to the Duke, and his bragging about it to Marta Vélez had only diminished his stature in her eyes.

The meeting taking place that afternoon would finalize the arrangements and protocol for how the Japanese Delegation would enter Sevilla: the route, security, who should be present, when and where. Input from the Duke, due to his close relations with the King and as a singular representative of Sevilla's high society, was considered crucial. Julian, in his own way, had actually cobbled together a program

that, whenever possible, looked to limit public contact and popular enthusiasm for the exotic guests. Leaving his friends late that
morning, he had counted on a meal, an assignation with Marta after
regaining her sympathies, and a rest before dressing suitably and arriving sober at the appointed chamber where Hasekura Tsunenaga
and Father Sotelo would be present.

But Marta had fled. Grief overwhelmed him. The thought of having to go on without the affections of his aunt was unbearable. A
relationship he had often seemed cavalier about and that he had
often assured himself he could walk away from was now something
he could not live without. He had managed to imagine it as being
only a satellite about his marriage to Guada, but now it meant more
to him than anything in the world. He saddled his horse and went
after her.

Three hours later, he caught up with her carriage between Lebrija
and Las Cabezas de San Juan. The carriage came to a halt by a stand
of azaleas near a farm where goats grazed in an adjacent field. The
goats were minded by a youth who leaned upon a walking stick to
watch the novel encounter. The carriage was green and gold and
drawn by four black horses. The young nobleman who had implored it to stop was dressed in sky-blue silken finery and rode an
Arabian stallion.

Marta Vélez refused to step down from the cabin, preferring to conduct the conversation through the lowered window with a veil covering her face. Upon accepting the fact she would not deign to leave
the carriage, Julian dismounted and asked, 'Why? Why have you
done this? Where are you going?'
    'I'm going home where I belong,' she said.

'But what's happened?'

'I'm tired, Julian.'

'Tired.'

'Of many things.'

'Tired of me?'

'Once again you disappoint me. A real man would not have come after me. A real man would have fulfilled his responsibility attending the meeting that was scheduled for an hour ago. Only a spoiled boy, a hapless scrounger unworthy of his title and inheritance, would have shamed himself by following me instead of doing his duty.'

A sword driven through his heart would not have pained him more.

'You mock my affection for you.'

'The affection of which you speak has run its course and come to an end. It was there, once upon a time, we embraced it, unwisely I'm sure, but now it's been used up.'

'Not for me.'

'You must grow up, Julian. Abandon your boring, illiterate, unattractive friends. Return to your wife and give her children. Take care of your estates. Honor the King.'

'I cannot face my wife unless I have you.'

'Then find another, or another me. There are many of us, I fear.'

'There is someone else, isn't there?'

'Julian,' she said, attempting to inject a tone of kindness into her voice, which only made him more desperate, 'let us end on a better note.'

She knocked upon the carriage wall to signal for the driver to proceed.

'Who is it?' he said to her in a fury.

'No one,' she said. 'And in any case, it is no longer your concern.'

As the carriage pulled away, he filled with rage, the rage of humiliation, self-abasement, and pain. He drew his dagger and threw it at the rear of the carriage. He hoped to at least hear the stinging thud of its impalement into the fragile wood, hoped that she too would hear it and see it upon her arrival. But it missed its mark and disappeared into a rut of mud and grass. Julian swung up into the saddle and crudely spurred his horse, turning it around to return to Sanlúcar, where he had no intention of spending another night in all his life.

Once the aristocrats had gone, the goatherd boy descended the hill and made his way onto the road that had been traced by Roman legions centuries earlier. He found the dagger easily and marveled at its quality. He stuck it in his belt as a trophy and proof for the tale he would tell that evening to his father and brothers.

– XVIII –

In which anger rises and a secret is revealed

Guada was assigned a new handmaiden, a plain-looking girl, somewhat plump, overly servile, of meager education, and destined for the convent. Guada found in her an ideal companion with whom to spend long hours praying for guidance within the Duke's chapel, or to stroll beside in his well-tended gardens, gardens turned romantically somber by the autumn damp and the fallen quinces that rotted uncollected upon the mossy earth. These latter excursions only took place when she knew that Shiro and the Duke were off hunting in the mountains.

Days later, her mother arrived, and as soon as it was possible to attain some privacy, Guada proceeded to share all that had happened during the journey to the sea and back, all save for the first evening's walk with the foreigner. The horror and shock that registered on the visage of Doña Inmaculada when she heard of the Duke's plan to wed a married commoner from the village was only equaled by the giddy thrill that passed back and forth between mother and daughter, a thrill kept barely at bay by repeated declarations of '*Madre mia*,' '*Qué vergüenza*,' and '*No me lo puedo creer*.'

On the very day they returned from the sea, the Duke installed Rosario at the finca in a private suite of rooms and summoned her husband for a face-to-face meeting. After obligatory spasms of protest, Antonio, as hirsute and slight of stature as Rosario had described, accepted the Duke's terms with avaricious speed. Letters were dispatched to the Holy See, to Cardinal Bernardo de Rojas y Sandoval, and to the King. And a letter was waiting for the Duke, written by the mayor of Sanlúcar, expressing doubts about the efficacy of the young emissaries the Duke had sent to engage with the foreign delegation from Japan. As the Duke read, and recalled what Shiro had said on the first day they met, he could only imagine how grievous the behavior of Julian and his nephews had been. He sent the mayor a note of thanks and reassurance, along with a message for the mayor to hand-deliver to Hasekura Tsunenaga in which he apologized while making a point of not mentioning his own deepening friendship with the young Samurai.

Offering one excuse and then another, Guada had been able to avoid taking meals with the Duke, Shiro, and Rosario since their return, trying the Duke's patience. His initial sympathy and weakness for the girl had altered. Part of him still hoped that behind her religiosity, reserve, and shyness there hid a creature of passion, but another part of him now wondered if she might be just as limited and dull as she often chose to appear. She finally showed her face at the dinner table on the evening of Doña Inmaculada's arrival.

The Duke and Rosario sat at opposite ends of the table. At one side, Guada and her mother sat next to each other facing Shiro, who had the other side to himself. This seating arrangement proposed a significant challenge to mother and daughter. Distraught with discomfort, neither of them wished to look at Rosario. When obliged to listen or respond to her, they cast their eyes down at their plates or looked past her with unconvincing smiles. But neither did they wish to stare across at the young Japanese man who wore white that evening with a black sash. Doña Inmaculada's breeding did not permit her to ogle the novel foreigner who, she had learned in gory detail, had decapitated a Christian soldier with such bravura. Guada refused to look at him out of shame. The end result of all this ruffled femininity driven by codes of conduct common to the upper echelons of Sevilla society was that the two women spent an inordinate amount of time directing their dark-blue and hazel-green eyes at the Duke, who, with each passing minute, regarded them with expressions of mounting anger.

'Enough!' he finally blurted, banging a fork-filled fist upon the table.

All three female hearts stood still. Then it was Rosario's turn to look away. Shiro, not insensitive to the tensions prevailing in the house since the incident with the soldier, looked at all four of the barbarians with keen interest. What he most noticed, and it would stay with him long after the Duke's terrible tirade had passed, was how Guada's face blushed and lit up with fear, a combination that made her even more beautiful.

'I've had my fill,' the Duke continued. 'Could two women be more provincial?'

'I beg your pardon,' an offended Doña Inmaculada replied.

'It's too late for that,' he said, with biting sarcasm. 'I will not have my fiancée insulted any further.'

'I assure you,' Inmaculada said, her own anger awakening, 'we have no such intention.'

'You can't even look at her,' he said. 'You can't pronounce her name. It seems you feel some God-given superiority. It seems you've been living within the stifling confines of Sevilla for too long. Look at my ancestors, my father's mother, Ana de Aragón y Gurrea was a bastard child of the Archbishop of Zaragoza, who in turn was the bastard son of King Ferdinand the Second. And it seems you've forgotten who your own ancestors are, peering back just a few generations, one a sheep herder, one a blacksmith, one a thief incarcerated for life, one a tanner of animal hides.'

'I refuse to listen to such nonsense,' Inmaculada said. 'And besides, it's not that, or that only. For God's sake man, the girl is married. The girl's an adulterer and lives in mortal sin.'

These words affected the Duke in a manner Shiro found surprising. Rather than provoke an escalation of his cholera, it was as if the Duke felt a weight alighting from his soul.

'I imagine you both speak with your husbands from time to time,' he said in a much calmer tone.

'What, pray, might that have to do with anything?' Inmaculada asked.

'I suppose you even feel some affection for them,' he continued. 'I'm told that you, Guada, seem to think you are madly in love with Don Julian.'

She prayed the ground might open beneath her chair and swallow her, drag her into a dark abyss, anything to halt this hellish meal.

'Surely,' the Duke continued, 'you both know that Rodrigo, your husband Inma, your beloved father Guada consorts regularly with other women, which, unless he has received some special dispensation from the Pope that I have yet to learn of, makes him an adulterer, a man living as you say in mortal sin.'

Rosario bit at the insides of her mouth, doing all she could to suppress a most inopportune grin. Shiro made himself a promise to study further this barbarian concept of sin that seemed to trip from their lips with such frequency. Clearly the catechism he'd been made to study had not done it justice. The Duke closed in for the kill.

'But something that neither of you is aware of perhaps, something I myself have known for some time and could not care less about because it only relates to the sort of natural animal behavior I very much doubt our Lord in heaven notices at all, is that both of your husbands have been 'sinning' with the same woman, the rather nasty but undeniably attractive Marta Vélez.'

As blood rose reddening her cheeks, Doña Inmaculada rose from the table. Guada, beginning to cry, remained seated.

'What a sinister side of yourself you've shown me,' Inmaculada spat at the Duke. 'Now I understand how you might seek the favors of a village wench to flatter you in your fast-approaching senility.'

Before the battling aristocrats could further vitiate their venom, both were silenced when Guada finally spoke through her tears.

'I know about this woman, with respect to Julian. But I can assure you they no longer see each other, that since we celebrated the Holy Sacrament of Matrimony he has been free of sin in that regard.'

Though part of him felt for her and took pity on her, most of him disdained her then, and he marveled at the magnitude of their delusions and hypocrisy. 'I can assure you, sweet Guada, you for whom I had the dearest affection before you chose to disparage the woman I love, a woman who has done you no harm, you, whose grace I hope to see one day regained, I can assure you that your Julian is having his way with his aunt, the Señora Vélez, this very moment. Why do you think he left your side so easily and has stayed in Sanlúcar so much longer than called for?'

She looked at him in anger, as if struck.

'That is a lie!'

The Duke gestured with his chin toward Shiro.

'You saw them together, did you not?'

'I did, sir,' the Samurai replied.

Her faced transformed into a marsh of tears. She stood and clung to her mother, who was still reeling from the shock of these revelations.

'And as for the regrettable and erroneous marriage Rosario entered into and about which I care not a wit, that is being seen to,' said the Duke. 'As soon as I have it annulled, and annulled it shall be, we will marry, not to please the eyes of God or to silence the wicked tongues of the villagers and of your own rancid class in Sevilla—my own people whom I shrink from more and more with each passing day—but as a gift to her so that, upon my demise, she shall be well provided for.'

Though mother and daughter heard all that he said, for the dining hall though large was rife with hard surfaces including large slabs of black-and-white Carrera marble covering the floor, they had almost exited the room by the time he was finished. The Duke then proceeded to apologize to Rosario and to Shiro, and all agreed that family relations were among the most difficult to manage regardless of where one breathed upon the Earth.

Later in the evening, Shiro attempted to see Guada in the hope he might cheer her, might explain himself and express regret at the

Duke's revelation about something he assumed would remain in confidence. In truth, he simply wished to see her. But she would not see him. The new handmaiden, forced to confront the foreigner at close range and incapable of believing he dominated the Castilian language, delivered her lady's refusal repeatedly, in loud tones, assuming that increased volume was more efficacious than clear diction.

Turning away, Shiro realized how weary he was of his Christians. Ignoring the lateness of the hour, he left the finca and set out upon a narrow path up into the hills. The silence of the countryside was cleansing. The earth was damp. The air was cold and clear and tinged with the smell of chimney smoke. And he was comforted to note that the constellations shining above were the same ones he'd often gazed upon from the balconies of the Sendai Castle.

– XIX –

In which a gift is given

Three days later, the Duke, Shiro, Doña Inmaculada, and Guada, along with an impressive complement of guards, cooks, and servants, set out for Sevilla. Rosario, without the slightest regret, stayed behind. Unbeknownst to all, she had conceived a child in Baelo Claudia. Now that their relationship was out in the open, the Duke was distraught to leave her, but he was eager as well to greet the Japanese Delegation and to see a dear friend. Shiro was not averse to rejoining his fellow Samurais. Inmaculada and her daughter were perhaps the most desirous to return to their respective homes, though their eagerness was strongly tempered by the prospect of confronting their husbands.

A certain degree of peace had been regained. Inmaculada and Guada had comforted each other, prayed together, and grown closer. They found a common bond in the shared pain of betrayal. It had been one thing for Doña Inmaculada to know that Rodrigo had dalliances with other women, but quite something else to have a particular woman singled out and identified who was not a common prostitute, but a known member of her own society. Guada was bereft and furious with herself for having maintained the naive illusion that once Julian was able to enter her bed, he would forget the wiles of his vile aunt. Inmaculada had even mustered enough tact to approach

Rosario and apologize for her and her daughter's behavior, blaming entrenched and perhaps outdated social mores as the culprit.

But she was unable to convince her daughter to do the same. In all the time Guada and Rosario had spent together, the latter had never taken the former into her confidence, and it was clear to Guada that she had been used as a conduit through which her handmaiden had been able to sin without raising suspicion. And the betrayal went deeper. Guada's exposure to the attentions of Shiro at the beach combined with the flagrant licentiousness going on within the neighboring tent at night had deeply unsettled her.

But by the time the group left for Sevilla, most of everyone's jagged nerves had calmed considerably. On the second day of the journey, Doña Inmaculada mounted sidesaddle and joined the Duke at the head of the column. Shiro took advantage and tied his horse to the carriage where Guada rode and successfully got himself invited to sit within.

'I've been meaning to explain myself to you,' he said, 'for the discomfort I caused you by confirming the Duke's assertion the other night.'

'There's no need for that,' she said, not quite looking at him.

He sat facing her. The space was confined, the road uneven. Jostled to and fro, their knees grazed against each other with every rut and stone. The awareness of their physical proximity made it difficult to concentrate. She wore brown boots and a brown silk dress with white cuffs and collar that accentuated her blond hair and green eyes. About her neck hung a simple locket he admired, and he noticed a chipped nail on her left index finger. He kept his hands hidden whenever possible, ashamed in such close quarters by his extra digit. The lean strength he emanated, the simplicity of his robe, the directness of his open and, what she could not deny was a comely, gaze, combined with the memory of how he had responded to her silent plea days before, all contributed to an acceleration of her heart despite her effort to control it.

'Nevertheless,' he said.

She grabbed a leather strap affixed by the window and stared out at the forests of oak and eucalyptus and at newly plowed fields of dark soil that graced the outskirts of a village called Espera.

'The greatest "discomfort," as you call it, I felt that night and which I cannot shake free of, was the pain of humiliation—with myself.' These last two words she uttered looking directly at him before looking away again. 'I should have been more cynical and realistic. I've behaved like a child.'

The mixture of her strength and delicacy, her coloring, the reality of her body being so close disturbed him.

'You are in love,' he said.

'I was,' she answered, trying not to cry again, fixing her gaze upon a colorful pair of bee-eater birds alighting on a nearby tree.

He was stunned to hear it and provoked by it, but he attempted to diminish it.

'It's too soon to know that,' he said.

She looked at him. 'What is it with men?'

'I do not understand,' he said.

'Your need to pounce upon women, the feverish pursuit, the unsightly slobbering.'

Though unable to take his eyes off of her, he felt unjustly accused.

'Not all men are alike,' he said.

She stared at her hands and began to pick at the damaged nail. She ignored his comment and went on. 'I mean in the case of my father I find it more understandable. My mother refuses him and has for a long time. This other woman is of his class and is his junior and, or so I have heard, is caught within a bad marriage. But Julian . . .'

Shiro would do nothing to aid the cause of the young noble who had insulted him back in Sanlúcar, and he remained silent.

'You must think us all mad,' she said, feeling self-conscious about her nail and pulling on the pair of yellow kid gloves folded upon her lap. 'You've only recently arrived, and here you are thrust into the midst of so much soiled linen.'

This expression, a colloquialism she often used with friends and family, spoken to a man from so distant a culture, suddenly revealed its literal meaning to her, and once again she felt herself reddening, this time with embarrassment.

'Soiled linen is not unique to your country,' he said, smiling at her.

She prayed to God he was either familiar with or had grasped the metaphor.

'I suspect it is so common,' he added, 'regardless of whether you might consider it sinful or not, that I would hesitate to introduce the word "soiled." It seems to simply be part of human nature.'

The statement was promising, but still, she could not be sure. 'How do you mean?' she asked.

'The Lord I serve where I come from is like a King. His blood flows through my veins, and he has told me that I am a Prince because of it. But my mother, his only sister, after losing her husband in battle, conceived me with another man, another Prince of sorts, who was already married and who had other sons. I might thus be considered an article of soiled linen.'

'I had no idea,' she said.

'And yet, despite some rough treatment from cousins and half siblings, I have been well cared for. Though not ideal, my condition is not so uncommon, and the honor of my bloodlines are known to all. I would even go as far as to say my upbringing, my status as an outsider among the rest, has been more advantageous to my character than otherwise. It has given me more freedom with which to make my own life, untethered to the stricter rules and responsibilities that weigh upon my 'cleaner relations.''

Rather than offending or alienating her, the admission of his condition as a bastard only increased his attractiveness, a sensation she felt then and there without dissimulation. And yet she could not explain it.

'What you confess to . . .' she said, 'I am grateful for it. Is the Duke appraised of your tale?'

'He has been appraised of it since the first day we met.'

They sat in silence listening to the creaking wheels of the carriage.

'I would like to give you something,' he said.

'There is no need for that.'

'It would please me to do so. It is a small thing.'

From the folds of his robe he took out the small envelope his mother had given him back in Sendai. He opened it and poured some of the *Biwa* seeds into his hand to keep for himself. Then he handed the envelope to Guada.

'These are seeds for a fruit tree I have yet to see here. My mother gave them to me. It would give me great pleasure if you might plant them. In Japanese, the fruit is called a Biwa. It grows to be the size of a lemon but looks like a peach and is pleasant to the taste and has medicinal properties and a beautiful blossom.'

She took the envelope. He enjoyed seeing it in her hand.

'Thank you,' she said.

Their encounter was interrupted by the return of Doña Inmaculada to the carriage. Giving in to maternal instinct upon seeing the two youths together unchaperoned, she felt an urge to intervene. Shiro bid Guada adieu with a curt bow and left to make room for her mother. Rapidly freeing and remounting his horse, he caught up once again to the Duke, who, even on dry ground, looked every bit the Admiral of the High Seas.

'How fares the stubborn little Princess?' the Duke asked.

'Well,' Shiro replied. 'Better.'

'Her mother has been endeavoring to soften my attitude, but until the girl apologizes for her rudeness, I shall pay her little heed no matter how much it pains me.'

'In my heart I am sure she shall see the error of her ways,' Shiro said.

'I suspect the provenance of your certainty derives from another part of your anatomy. But tell me,' he added, not averse to changing the topic, 'what will become of you once you rejoin your people in Sevilla?'

'I shall do my best to blend in, to keep my eyes on Hasekura Tsunenaga from afar, and to see more of your country. We will travel soon to Madrid, where Hasekura Tsunenaga plans to meet with your King and finally take the Christian sacrament of Baptism in his presence.'

'But are his beliefs more genuine than yours?'

'In truth I do not know, but I would not rule it out. He is close to the Spanish priest Father Sotelo and it was Hasekura Tsunenaga who insisted we Samurai make our conversion upon landing in New Spain.'

'I've no desire to interfere with your responsibilities, but I would like to keep you close to me, first in Sevilla where your skill at translation will be crucial to me, but in Madrid, as well, at court, where I shall be able to make your stay more comfortable and amusing. It will please me to do so.'

And so, as the afternoon began to cede its place to evening, as the high cliffs of Arcos de la Frontera loomed in the distance, the white village, its trees soon to be pruned, the fields they rode between plowed or covered with new grass, they conversed in their saddles, a couple as odd and unlikely as the one described by Cervantes in his still unfinished work.

– XX –

In which the Samurais arrive in Sevilla

Shiro's absence from Sanlúcar de Barrameda had barely been noted. His Samurai brethren were too distracted adjusting to the easygoing rhythms of Andalusian society while doing their best to maintain discipline. Whenever Hasekura Tsunenaga realized that Date Masamune's bastard nephew was still missing, it was a source of satisfaction. Even Father Sotelo, who admired the young Samurai with stirrings of unholy lust, was too occupied, putting his master plan into effect. When not conferring with and counseling Hasekura Tsunenaga, he was busy composing and dispatching letters to Madrid and Rome, promoting the delegation as if it were his own. He pled for audiences and patronage and was busy finagling to obtain a sliver of the Holy Cross to take back to Japan, where it would be enclosed within a golden crucifix that he imagined adorning the main altar of the cathedral he hoped to build and preside over. Then, following the towns lined along the river, they began the short journey north toward Sevilla.

Julian had only just arrived there. Bored, prickly, and resentful, he had returned to the mansion bequeathed to him and Guada upon their marriage. As he was unable to argue for the somber and limited reception for the Japanese Delegation he had planned to present on the day Marta Vélez abandoned him, others had prevailed. Their concept for the event was considerably more generous and festive.

On the appointed day, the streets were lined with sevillanos of all descriptions: aristocrats, gypsies, merchants, functionaries of the crown and officials from the Archive of the Indies, members of numerous religious orders along with droves of women and children. Palm trees and flowering magnolia trees glistened under a warm October sun. Parasols in pastel hues rose and fell along the Triana Bridge as the exotic procession crossed the Guadalquivir on horseback en route to the Alcázar gardens, where a reception awaited them. Representing the king, the Duke was there to proclaim their official welcome. He'd sent word prohibiting Julian and his two nephews from attending. When Shiro asked someone about the origins of the unusual architecture surrounding them in the Alcázar gardens, he was treated to a lecture about the Moors and Islam, causing his head to spin at the realization there was yet another complex faith in the world rife with more rules and restrictions he would have to study.

The Duke accepted Father Sotelo's obsequious offer to translate during the opening ceremonies, the toasts, and the exchange of gifts. But once Hasekura Tsunenaga expressed a desire to speak with the Duke in private, the Grandee of Spain called for Shiro.

Father Sotelo stared at the Duke in puzzlement. 'Shiro, my Lord?' said the priest, doing all he could to maintain a smile for the sake of Hasekura Tsunenaga, 'I do not recommend it.'

Accustomed to clergymen from good families with whom he might exchange a pleasantry or two about mutual relatives, the Duke found this man, a commoner, to be a nuisance.

'And why is that?' he asked.

'The Ambassador has chosen me as his official translator. Have I been remiss in any way?'

'Not that I can tell, padre, but then, how would I know? Let me propose, no, insist, on the following compromise. You shall continue to translate for His Excellency the Ambassador, and Shiro shall translate for me.'

The priest related the Duke's words to Hasekura Tsunenaga, who responded in Japanese with something short and gruff.

'His Excellency wonders why you have chosen an inexperienced young man for such a delicate task?' asked the priest.

'Tell His Excellency,' the Duke replied, 'that I do it to honor his good judgment. I can only assume that the Samurai chosen to travel all the way to my ancestral home to convey His Excellency's greetings must be one he holds in particular esteem.'

– XXI –

In which sorrow prepares a crime

Guada found Julian in the library. He was pretending to review papers related to their estates. He had given his footman instructions to alert him the minute his wife came through the front door. He wished to appear manly and serious, the responsible custodian of their properties and holdings. The brief minute he spent actually looking at the documents while she climbed the marble stairs numbed his brain with boredom and befuddlement. He found the legal language their assessors employed impenetrable. Once certain she had seen and appreciated his *tableau vivant*, he feigned to notice her and rose from the desk.

'My Lady.'
    'Husband.'
    Polite pairs of kisses were aimed at cheeks not reached.
    'I trust you had a safe journey,' he said.
    'Safe as safe can be, but long, and frightfully uncomfortable.'
    'You must rest and then we can dine, whenever you wish.'

She determined a bath was in order, and after it, glistening from scented oil, she regarded herself in a large mirror that leaned against the whitewashed wall. She was in her prime. Unable to remember the last time she had observed herself with such critical frankness, she was taken aback, experiencing satisfaction and blushing shame simultaneously.

It was evening by then, and cold meats were served with eggs fried in oil with bread to dip into the oil and the yolk. He, but not she, rubbed his bread with garlic. He drank a concoction brewed especially for him that was akin to ale, and she took water stained with brandy. Once the food and drink were served, the servants retreated to an adjacent chamber.

'You've said nothing of your stay in Sanlúcar,' she said.

'I haven't had the chance, and, in truth, there is not much to tell,' he replied.

'But I understand the task the Duke entrusted to you was important, and I remember the pleasure it gave you to set forth from Medina-Sidonia, a pleasure I found most hurtful.'

'Though a noble in my own right,' he said, with what he hoped she would regard as a rakish grin, 'to be favored by the Duke of Medina-Sidonia is a considerable honor. The pleasure you recall derived exclusively from that.'

'And yet,' she said, her voice beginning to rise, 'you did so good a job of it that you've been banned from the reception the Duke is holding for the Delegation you were charged with.'

She could see color entering his cheeks that matched her own. 'I rather think,' she went on, 'the pleasure you felt at the thought of leaving me had more to do with the satisfaction it gave you to lie to me on so bold a scale, to renege on the solemn promise you made before we married, the perversity you looked forward to, your continuing lust for your haggard aunt.'

The fury he had swallowed owing to his abandonment by Marta Vélez, a fury that had only recently begun to subside, came to life again with a jolt and was joined by more fury still: at himself for being found out, and at Guada. He pushed his chair back, its legs scraping against the marble floor, and stood up.

"How dare you accuse me of such a thing!"

'How dare you deny it!' she said. 'Did you really think you could get away with such a flagrant transgression while surrounded by men whose livelihoods depend upon the Duke's largesse?'

'Your jealousy is as misguided as it is unbecoming. You should be ashamed,' he said, raising and shaking his index finger in the air.

"So you are denying it?"

"Absolutely."

"When mother and I showed our displeasure the other night at the Duke's decision to marry an already wed village girl, he retaliated by telling us about your escapades and drunken revelries, and your incompetence as a diplomat."

He stormed over to where she sat and struck her across the face.

"Silence, woman! That will be enough."

No one had ever struck her.

'Silence? Woman?' she laughed aloud, tears in her eyes, a rivulet of blood upon her lip. 'I've known you all my life, Julian. And you're still a boy. A boy with a problem I naively thought I could solve once I let you into my bed. What is it this woman has that both my father and you find so irresistible? She cannot be fairer than I or more generous in her exertions. My father has the excuse of being married to a woman who no longer admits him to her boudoir, but you do not.'

He raised his hand to strike her again. As he did so she used her forearms to cover her face, beginning to sob.

'Do you remember what you told me one night before we were married' he said, softening his tone. "I marry you freely, you as you are," you said. "I have come to treasure your heart, your heart with all its complications and extraneous attachments," you said. "Trust me, you said, and you shall see of what I speak.'

'You broke your promise,' she cried out, her head turned away.

He walked out of the room, retrieved his cloak and sword downstairs, and left the massive house for the nearest tavern. He wished to tell her how his sins with his aunt had come to an end but realized how little it would do to improve the villainy already revealed. The only thing that gave him any sense of purpose that night as he drank with abandon was the thought of exacting revenge. Surely it had been the lowly sailor, the filthy one-armed rogue who had accompanied the savage Asian to Medina-Sidonia, the foul-smelling sevillano he had actually paid to remain silent.

– XXII –

In which a wife becomes a widow

Apart from the unsettling coincidence that her son-in-law's mistress and her husband's were one and the same, Doña Inmaculada was not especially perturbed by the news that Rodrigo was seeing a noblewoman. Not only a noblewoman, but one well regarded at court. Over the years, her fantasies concerning the satisfaction of Rodrigo's baser needs had led her to conjure up brothels blackened with grime and populated by women unmannered and unclean. She was grateful Rodrigo was in Madrid that week, allowing her respite and time to consider whether her newly gained knowledge was worth throwing in his face.

For a moment, she entertained the notion that perhaps they visited the woman together. But she presumed to know her husband well enough to eliminate such a possibility. At the very least, he was too vain and, in his way, too old-fashioned. The idea, in fact, just before she banished it forever, caused her to giggle aloud.

The most scandalous and irritating part of the sordid tale for her was that the Duke knew about it. Worse yet, that most disagreeable and vociferous argument had been carried out in front of Guada and Rosario and the peculiar stranger. But somehow it had fostered a new sort of intimacy with the Duke. The cathartic repast had left a wearisome but welcome calm in its aftermath.

And with respect to Rodrigo, the Duke had done her a favor. What had constituted a tidal flow of speculation now had a name and a face. And though she would never admit it to anyone, it was someone she might get used to. She assumed he was with her now, and the thought, for the first time, allowed her to truly enjoy her solitude.

The only thorn remaining was Julian. Soledad Medina had warned them, and Guada it seemed, had been apprised of the young man's other attachment. Her daughter had reckoned with it, or so she had thought, with dignity. Guada's only error had been an excess of pride, believing him when he swore he would stop. The young man's weakness for his own aunt, half-aunt to be exact, combined with the poor reviews awarded his assignment in Sanlúcar, tested the bounds of Inmaculada's goodwill toward him. But some remained. She wished to look upon him after all as a son. Her own had been far more troubling to them thus far. Julian's faults were ones she could understand. And he was wealthy, and handsome, and his standing would surely improve with time and he would give Guada beautiful children. Yes, she thought, with sufficient patience and prayer, a way could be found to carry on and overcome these disappointing days.

***

When Diego Molina rode to Sevilla after leaving Shiro at the Duke's estate in Medina-Sidonia, he presented himself at the door of the Sánchez Ordoñez family. The abode was a modest house in the Triana district. Their prized daughter, Rocío Sánchez, had remained faithful to Diego for the two and a half years he had been at sea.

Though she only received three letters from him in all that time and was ardently pursued by a baker of means, her flame for Diego remained lit and constant.

The reunion was a joyous one. With the exception of his missing hand, Rocío found him even handsomer than she remembered, and with the exception of an additional kilo or two thanks to the baker's fruitless favors, he found in her a delectable answered prayer.

Upon payment by the bursar for his time at sea, he had twice the money he would have earned working with his family in the olive trade. But much more valuable from Rocío's point of view was his declaration that his wanderlust was sated, his avarice for adventure had becalmed. He told her that from then on the profession of selling harvests of choice arquebina olives would suit him just fine as long as he knew she would be there each evening with a meal and an embrace.

The wedding took place within a week of his arrival. They settled into a small, whitewashed house at the southern border of the olive estates in the countryside west of the city. They put their home in order and took pride going about their respective tasks. Enjoying home-cooked meals free of family and spending nights alone together went a long way toward eradicating the doubts and discomforts that had arisen during their separation. He regaled her with tales from his travels, and she filled him in on thirty months' worth of local gossip.

Then one day he did not return from the groves. A man he worked with only knew that a nobleman and two men had ridden into the fields asking for Diego. The man and Rocío spent the afternoon and evening walking up and down the carefully plowed hills of iron-rich soil where the olive trees had been planted by Phoenicians and Romans. As dusk settled, they were alerted by the barking of Diego's mastiff. They found the one-armed man on the verge of death, tied to a tree, run through by a sword. He was barely able to speak. They cut him down, and she rested his head upon her lap. She could not bear to look at the wound. After telling Rocío how much he loved her, and how sorry he was, his very last words were meant for someone else. 'Tell Shiro the Samurai,' he said, feeling the earth fall away from him, 'it was the noble who wrote the letter in Sanlúcar.'

She would not leave him. The man she came with went for help. She remained with the dog and her husband's body all through the night. She insisted he be buried where he lay, and when the priest objected, she spit at him. In silence she stayed by the tree and the mound where her man was interred for three days afterwards despite pleading from his family and her own. It was only when the baker came and sat down beside her that she deigned to speak. She looked at him with a fierceness he had never seen before. 'If you will take me to the Samurai,' she said—and he listened, not knowing what the word meant—'I shall marry thee before the year is out.'

– XXIII –

In which time stands still

Before taking leave of Sevilla to accompany the Japanese Delegation on their journey to Madrid, the Duke of Medina-Sidonia called on Soledad Medina. The Duke was fifty-seven years old that year, Doña Soledad, sixty. Eight years had passed since they had last seen each other at Guada's first holy communion.

The Duke first set eyes on Soledad at her wedding when, at seventeen, she married one of their older cousins, a popular but unpleasant fellow who early on had acquired a reputation as a philanderer and a boor. Only his wealth and the force of his personality had persuaded so many to put up with him. It was shortly after the obese and alcoholic brute died attempting to rape his game warden's daughter that the Duke and Soledad began their affair. He had always admired her beauty and elegance, her breeding and forbearance, and had felt sorry for the unfortunate choice her parents had made choosing her husband.

The Duke was married during those years, as well, but decorum required de rigueur that he take the occasional mistress. He was not prepared for Soledad Medina, for her erudition, wit, and ardor. The reality of his married life paled in comparison. What began as a dalliance deepened into an affair of the heart.

129

Though a widow by then, Soledad was subjected to a constant stream of warnings from friends and family. But for the first and last time in her life, she was deeply in love. The Duke teetered on the brink of leaving his wife. When Philip the Second insisted that the Duke take command of the Armada, some at court believed the sovereign's motive was mainly to douse the love affair with leagues of seawater in order to preserve noble decorum. True or not, it proved efficacious, for when the Duke returned to Spain, he was gray and sober, and after visiting Soledad one last time, he went back to his family.

That morning Soledad had spent an extra hour dressing and painting her face in preparation for his arrival. The Duke was moved by the effort and told her repeatedly how splendid and unchanged she looked. Though his limp was more pronounced, his hair thinner, his skin parched here and there, he was still, she thought, a handsome man.

'I'm told you are to be married,' she said with a smile, kissing him on both cheeks as a footman relieved the Duke of his cloak. She smelled of something citric, and he noted the softness of her cheeks, not the toned softness of yesteryear, but a frailer, powdery sort.

'I see tongues have been loosened,' he said.

'Inmaculada is my relation, too, and Guada the daughter I always wished for.'

'Well, then you know everything,' he said.

'Far from it,' she answered. 'All I have heard about is their horror, or their excitement disguised as horror. But what I wish to hear from you is how you've come to such a decision.'

"What can I say?"

They walked by salmon-hued columns under vaulted ceilings painted a lemony yellow that enclosed a large rectangular garden in whose center there murmured a simple, circular fountain. She led him into her breakfast room off the library, where white jasmine blossoms on slender vines twirled about the iron bars covering opened windows.

'I'd forgotten what a splendid house you have here,' he said, meaning it. 'This is the Sevilla I remember.'

'Out with it, man.'

'She makes me feel young. Her affections for me seem to be genuine. I wish to protect her.'

'And it humors you to force the rest of us to treat her as an equal.'

'That, too,' he said, laughing easily.

'Well, you must present me to her, and I shall throw you both a ball so that no one will ever say another word against her.'

'You're a true aristocrat, my dear. You should have moved to Paris long ago, where such sophistication is rewarded. You've been wasted and unappreciated in this narrow-minded alley.'

'Not by all, Alonso.'

A bottle of Manzanilla produced at one of her estates was brought in along with a plate of tortitas de camarón.

'Guada is upset,' she continued, wishing to remove a weight from her spirit.

'Upset with me?' he asked.

'Upset because you are so upset with her,' she answered.

'She behaved like a little provincial,' he said, but gently.

'That's what she is, man,' Soledad replied. 'But it is not her fault. This is how one learns. I'd hoped that staying with you might broaden her views some, but you were so harsh with her I'm afraid she's closed herself up more than ever.'

'Perhaps I was—and I shall apologize to her for it,' he said, eager to appear magnanimous and retain her regard. 'But I have to say she has gotten herself into a terrible marriage. The boy is insufferable, proud, sly, and stupid.'

'I do not doubt it,' she said, deferring to him. 'Perhaps I identify with her because of that, as well.'

'We were getting along beautifully except for when the husband was present, which is why I dispatched him to Sanlúcar as soon as I could. She is very pretty. She takes after you in that, as well.'

She opened her *abanico* as if to fan away the blush creeping up her neck, where wrinkles were kept from view by numerous strings of Mallorcan pearls.

'She needs an Alonso to come and rescue her,' she said, repeating his Christian name, 'to carry her off and show her true affection.'

'Well, she has a suitor already, and one I wholeheartedly endorse, one for whose gallantry I shall be eternally grateful. If it hadn't been for him, I wouldn't be sitting here.'

'Do tell.'

'And who tried,' he went on, 'with significant grace and tact, to court her while they were both under my roof. But all it did was tie her into knots.'

'Who?' she cried out, 'There must be some disadvantage to him you are keeping from me.'

'Not at all, except for the fact that he comes from a place located, I believe, on the other side of the World. He is even a Prince of sorts and a warrior, a knight if you will, something called a Samurai.'

She let out a yelp of surprise, leaning off to the side as she did so, a gesture he once knew well and had forgotten, and seeing it again made him smile.

'You cannot be serious,' she said. 'Do you mean he is one of those creatures in robes that paraded across the Guadalquivir the other day?'

'The very same,' he said. 'But this one is singular, and fine look-ing. I've grown to like him enormously. It's been an education. And he is mad for the girl, you can see it.'

'You can't be serious. It's too much. And Julian after all is one of us—and *very* handsome.'

'Is he?' he said, genuinely irritated. 'I hadn't noticed.'

'She's besotted with him. It will take more than the boy's incestu-ous infidelity and the attentions of a Samurai to pry her free.'

'I'm not so certain,' he said. 'I've been with them for almost two weeks and have observed them up close. Anyway,' he said, gesturing with his hand as if to swat a fly, 'enough of the young. They can sort it out on their own. They have time. I just wanted to see you and to inquire after you, my dear,' he said, taking her hand.

She looked at her hand in his and remembered when those same hands had been young and smooth and how once they had held on to each other possessed with love. Without letting go, they rose from their chairs and sat together on a simple wooden bench, a dark and austere piece of furniture more suited for a chapel, but softened by cushions covered in raw silk.

'I'm so pleased you've come to see me,' she said, her eyes filling with tears. 'You mustn't stay away from me for so long again.'

'I won't,' he said.

'Though just knowing you are alive,' she said, 'that you are still somewhere nearby, is sufficient.'

She squeezed his hand.

'And I am happy for you, for your new marriage,' she added.

– XXIV –

In which a Samurai strolls by a canal

The Duke and the Delegation set out for Madrid in early January. They rested two nights in Córdoba and then continued north toward Bailén before climbing for three days up through the steep forests of Despeñaperros that separate Andalucia from the meseta of La Mancha. In Almagro they stayed in German manor houses built and owned by associates of the Fugger family who ran the cinnabar mines. Riding past the wetlands of Daimiel, they observed flocks of falcons and purple heron. In Toledo they were put up in the Alcázar. And in Aranjuez, thanks to special permission obtained by the Duke, they were allowed to rest in the Royal Palace, though it was undergoing renovation and much of its exterior was draped in scaffolding.

In light of Shiro's relations with the Duke of Medina-Sidonia and Date Masamune, Father Sotelo had begun to treat the young Samurai with deference. Believing the Duke to be a religious man, he also erroneously deduced that the bond between Shiro and the Grandee of Spain included elements enriched by the Church. With this in mind and without wishing to alienate Hasekura Tsunenaga, he made a point of engaging the lad as often as he could throughout the journey north. Shiro saw through it, for subtlety was not part of the cleric's repertoire, but after he consulted with the Duke, they both agreed there would be no harm in humoring the priest.

On an afternoon in Aranjuez, Shiro and the Franciscan strolled together through one of the enormous royal gardens. They walked upon a path of flattened earth littered with fallen leaves that followed a canal of the River Tagus.

'Do you remember when first we met?' asked the priest.

There was something in the man's tone that irked the Samurai, a falseness, an unctuous flirtatiousness.

'I do,' Shiro said. He said it in Japanese, hoping to push the topic away.

'You were just a boy,' continued the priest in Spanish. 'And it is thanks to that and thanks to me that you speak my language so well and have thus managed to ingratiate yourself so successfully with a very powerful countryman of mine.'

'I had not put all of that together in my own mind,' Shiro said, returning to Spanish, as well, 'but I cannot deny the logic.'

'It's not, of course, that I am asking you to be grateful, as such, only . . .'

And here the priest faltered, as he realized it was in fact what he had intended. Shiro opted to help him out, finishing the sentence for him, '. . .only to point out, I'm sure, the unexpected turns with which life presents us.'

'Precisely.'

Shiro felt the man fidgeting and remembered how it had been to have him as a teacher, and he recalled how often the friar had preferred to hold his classes at the bathhouse within the Sendai Castle.

'Have you had, I wonder,' continued the priest, eager for a change of topic, 'an occasion to attend Mass with His Excellency during your sojourn in Medina-Sidonia?'

'I have,' Shiro replied, lying on instinct.

'And what was the village church like? I must confess I have never known the pleasure of visiting his ancestral town.'

'The interior of the church in the village, a fine specimen from without, with a bell tower that must command a splendid view, and located across the way from a convent from which the nuns never emerge, is unknown to me. For the Duke celebrates Mass, along with his family and guests, in his own chapel that is contiguous with his home.'

Shiro was doing his best to mimic the overly formal language the priest reveled in, that the man of humble origins employed believing it marked him as a well-educated gentleman of taste.

'Imagine that,' Sotelo said. 'I should, of course, have assumed as much. I only ask because I am hoping to build my own church, quite a large one, in Sendai.'

The concept bothered Shiro profoundly, but he did not let on.

'And I am hoping,' the priest continued, 'that once we reach Rome and have our audience with the Holy Father, I might prevail upon him to approve the idea.'

Shiro said nothing.

'I'm told the Pope is a good friend to the Duke of Medina-Sidonia.'

Amazed by the cleric's tactlessness, Shiro simply said, 'I understand. I shall do what I can.'

Upon hearing this, the priest halted with what he hoped was a dramatic flourish and put himself in front of Shiro as if to block his way. He took the Samurai's hands.

'I knew I could count upon you,' he said, his eyes widening with fervor. 'And I for my part shall do all I can to try and mend the tear between you and Hasekura Tsunenaga.'

'I am grateful for your offer,' Shiro replied, 'though I am not optimistic. If I were Hasekura Tsunenaga, I too would resent the presence of someone like myself, so much younger and, from his point of view, of lower birth. But I encourage you to assure him on my behalf, when you deem it appropriate, that we both desire the same thing, success, and that the barbarian Kings we meet will come to respect the names of Tokugawa Ieyasu and Date Masamune.'

'It will be my great pleasure,' the priest replied. And then he added, 'Do you miss Japan?'

'I do,' Shiro answered.

'You seem so at home here in my country, that I am almost surprised to hear it.'

'I am open to experience Father Sotelo, but let there be no mistake, I follow the Warrior's Way.'

The priest then took far too long to excuse himself, begging Shiro's pardon when he finally did, explaining that he had a meeting to attend with Hasekura Tsunenaga in order to review the final details of the ambassador's baptism that would soon take place in the presence of the King of Spain. Shiro noted the ecstasy with which the priest pronounced everyone's title and then watched as the Franciscan swayed like a duck, moving at last away from him back toward the royal household. The stained brown cassock was in need of laundering, and the man's sandals and dirty toes swished through the fallen leaves. He wondered if Lord Masamune knew of the scheming friar's plan for a church in Sendai, hoping and assuming he did not, hoping and assuming his Lord was prepared to go only so far in order to obtain treaties of trade with the barbarians.

There was something about the direction of the path he was on, with the canal flowing beside it, that reminded him of Date Masamune's private garden. He recalled his encounter with Yokiko and wondered how she might be faring. He wondered if he would ever see her again. Across the way there was a small wooded isle reachable by a narrow wooden bridge. On the isle, by a stand of chestnut trees, there stood a simple structure made of brick, with two windows and a slanting roof covered with slate tiles. There was no one else about. In his mind, Shiro transformed the elegant little shed that was probably a place to keep tools used by the royal gardeners into a Spanish version of the bungalow where Yokiko had waited for him after his bath. He imagined himself emerging from the canal, naked and refreshed, and entering the shed where a fire and Guada would be. How she would dry him off as Yokiko had.

He stopped short of the bridge, reluctant to continue. He decided not to cross it and thus destroy his dream. Instead, he leaned upon the stone parapet and looked across the way, listening to the water's movement and to the breeze moving the dead leaves about him.

***

Just as the sun began to set the following afternoon, the column of horses came to a halt. They were on a dusty road flanked by beige plains of rolling wheat stalks. Ahead of them in the distance, the land rose from the plains, becoming low hills that were dotted with trees pruned back for winter. At the top of the hills sat a massive castle where the city began.

The Duke pointed and spoke to Shiro and Hasekura Tsunenaga mounted on their horses beside him, 'There is Madrid. And there, upon the rise, its Alcázar, the King's palace.'

One week later on the same spot, Diego Molina's widow, Rocío Sánchez and her baker paused to take in the very same view.

– PART THREE –

– XXV –

In which we meet a King and a note is intercepted

It was snowing in the Sierra de Guadarrama just north of Madrid, where it had been raining for days. Water streamed down the gutters along the Calle del Arenal from the Royal Palace through the Puerta del Sol and raced down the steep incline of the Calle de Segovia toward the River Manzanares. Filth and sewage went with it, lending the capital, however temporarily, a patina of cleanliness.

It was the day Hasekura Tsunenaga and his Samurai were granted their first audience with the King of Spain. The Monarch was thirty-seven years old, a widow, and known as Philip the Third, or, to some, as Philip the Pious. On this occasion, announced by a herald as all who were present bowed down before him, he was called: 'His Majesty Philip the Third, by the grace of God, King of Castile, Leon, Aragon and the Two Sicilies, of Jerusalem and Portugal, of Navarre, Granada, Toledo, Valencia and Galicia, of the Mallorcas, of Seville, Cordoba, Corsica and Murcia, of Guinea and the Algarve, of Gibraltar and the Canary Islands, of the Eastern and Western Indies, the Islands of Terra Firma of the Ocean Sea, Archduke of Austria, Duke of Burgundy and Milan, Count of Habsburg, Barcelona, and Biscay, and Lord of Molina.'

The room in which the audience took place was enormous. The throne was elevated. Towering stained glass windows depicting religious themes cast a sullen palette of rainbow hues upon the cold floor stones. The only other light came from torches stuck into iron sconces.

The King was fair of complexion, not tall, and sported an orange-tinged mustache. In his left hand he held a pair of gloves. His right hand rested upon the hilt of a highly polished sword. Shiro counted as many priests in attendance as soldiers. There were no women. A cloud of incense hung thick in the air, and its scent clung to the high vaulted walls, as if to cover the odors of so many ill-washed men.

Shiro gazed upon the King, one of the two powerful men they had crossed the great oceans to meet with, and he wondered how many of his fellow Samurai, including Hasekura Tsunenaga, knew that the man had never raised a sword against anyone. Philip the Third's power and wealth, the almost unimaginable size of his domains, were incontrovertible. But he was not a warrior. Even the dour gentleman at his side, the First Duke of Lerma, whom Shiro's own Duke had told him about, a man who was feared and groveled to by most in the realm, was not a warrior, either. To Shiro, the idea that men not scarred by battle might order others into it was a novelty. He found it unmanly. The Tokugawa Shoguns, all of them, had earned their supremacy leading men into battle at the front of the line. His own Lord, Date Masamune, had lost an eye, a brother-in-law, and countless colleagues in hand-to-hand combat.

Given that the history of his own island nation went back just as far, the young Samurai could not glean any correlation between this King who did not fight and the age of his empire. But perhaps it did have something to do with size. It was said that in China, after a millennium of struggle, the Emperors were raised from an early age to spend their days much as the King before him probably did: surrounded by guards willing to shed their blood for him, by squinting advisors badly remunerated who did the grueling work of administration, and by doctors who spent their mornings studying the Sovereign's stool. According to what he had learned from speaking with the Duke, the early leaders of Rome had been fighters, military men, and generals. But as time went on and their empire grew large and fat with wealth and complicated by the strains of keeping control over so many disparate lands and peoples, its leadership became hereditary, as well, and the Roman Emperors no longer wielded swords.

Hasekura Tsunenaga presented the Christian King with a letter written in the hand of Date Masamune. It conveyed the Lord's most heartfelt greetings and salutations. It asked for a treaty of trade and encouraged more Christian missionaries to visit Sendai.

The herald held the letter that was an opened scroll, as Father Sotelo, translating, read it aloud with Hasekura Tsunenaga at his side. As the King listened, he noticed that the Duke of Medina-Sidonia and a young Samurai with pleasing features were near enough to peer at the scroll, as well. After it was rolled shut and retied and handed to the King but taken by the Duke of Lerma, the King declared that he would gladly take the requests under consideration. Then he addressed Hasekura Tsunenaga directly through Father Sotelo.

'Is it true that all of your men have been baptized upon landing in New Spain?'

'Yes Your Majesty.'

The King looked about at his courtiers and began to clap until every other Christian in the room joined in.

'And is it true that you yourself shall be baptized here with us in Madrid?'

'Yes Your Majesty,' replied the priest.

This led to more clapping. When it died down, the Duke of Lerma spoke, looking first at the King and then at Hasekura Tsunenaga.

'The ceremony shall take place on the 17th of February in the Monasterio de las Descalzas Reales. My brother, the Archbishop of Toledo, will perform the rite. I shall be your godfather and the King your witness.'

This elicited thunderous applause. During it, the King gave the Duke of Medina-Sidonia a smile and a nod and stared again at Shiro.

Everyone was then invited into an adjacent hall where a reception took place in honor of the foreigners. This chamber was even larger than the first, and brighter. It was filled with paintings and lined with a continuous row of clear windows overlooking wet gardens and the narrow river far below. The Duke of Medina-Sidonia's oldest son and heir, Juan Mañuel, was there along with his wife, Juana de Sandoval, who was the daughter of the Duke of Lerma. Also present were Guada's father, Don Rodrigo, and Marta Vélez. Shiro observed how in this room another side of the King emerged. Having concluded his business, the Monarch no longer appeared interested in conversing further with Hasekura Tsunenaga and the unctuous Franciscan, preferring instead to gossip with those he knew.

The Duke of Medina-Sidonia, along with his son, his daughter-in-law, and Shiro, approached the King and the Duke of Lerma. Before the Admiral of the High Seas could offer his formal greetings, the King spoke first.

'I understand congratulations are in order, Alonso.'

'Your Majesty?'

'I received your letter, your upcoming nuptials, or have you changed your mind?'

'No I have not, and thank you, Sire.'

'She must be quite special indeed.'

'That she is, Your Majesty. But there is still the question of an annulment.'

'Details,' said the King. 'We shall work it out. But why marry her at all, man? You've already got your heir here. You and I have done our duty to God and country. Since the Queen passed away, I've never once considered remarriage. It seems to me, and with the blessings of God, that we now deserve the pleasure of variety, do we not?'

The Duke of Lerma, thought to be even more pious than his liege, reacted with a somber scowl, pretending to disapprove of a view he heartily shared in private. The scowl was also meant to show some solidarity with what he assumed his daughter might be thinking.

'I've known the variety you speak of, Your Majesty' said the Duke of Medina-Sidonia. 'And I've tired of it. It seems at heart I am a romantic.'

'Well put, Alonso,' said the King. 'If you do not invite me to the ceremony I shall be very put out.'

'It will be an honor.'

'It is an example to us all,' said the King, 'to see a man your age, still . . . how shall I put it . . . gallivanting. Juan Mañuel, what do you think of your father's engagement?'

'I will be glad to see him accompanied at this stage of his life,' the son replied. 'I know my mother would have wished it for him as well.'

'A fine sentiment,' said the King. 'Have you met the young woman?'

'I have not, Your Majesty. Not yet.'

'He's been keeping her from you. Probably wise.'

Then he looked at Juana de Sandoval. 'Watch out for this one, Doña Juana, if he starts to take after his father, you'll have to chain him down.'

The Duke of Lerma felt a twinge, and his mustache suddenly itched, worried that his daughter, whom he did not know very well, might stammer or respond with something too serious. He needn't have been concerned.

'If it comes to that, Your Majesty,' she said, 'I shall make sure to affix the chain to where most it pains.'

She knew this was just the sort of thing the King relished.

'Ouch!' exclaimed the Monarch.

'Alonso,' he then said, 'Who is this young man at your side from the Japanese Delegation?'

'This is Shiro San Your Majesty, a Prince, directly related to Date Masamune, the author of the letter read aloud to you this morning.'

Shiro bowed, and the King was pleased.

'He is also fluent is our language,' the Duke continued, 'taught as a boy by the Franciscan priest.'

'Most impressive. How do you like Spain, young man?'

'I am entranced, Your Majesty, and today more than ever, for the honor of your company of course, but as well because of these extraordinary paintings. They are like nothing I have ever seen.'

'But surely painters ply their craft in your country.'

'They do, Your Majesty, but with a very different style and technique. I have never seen such naturalism, such depth of color. I am astonished.'

'You are an aesthete, I see.'

'He is also a devil with a sword,' said the Duke. 'He saved my life with it last month.'

'Is that so,' said the King, 'an unusual combination indeed. Tell me, Shiro San, what convinced you to convert to our faith, to become a Catholic?'

'I believe what most persuaded me was the Christian concept of forgiveness.'

'Ah yes,' the Monarch replied. 'A fine answer, and a thing far easier to preach than practice.'

Shiro bowed again.

'I hope we get to see more of you,' the King concluded.

Shiro was forced to amend his first impression of the Monarch. The ease with which the King exercised his power was novel, his relaxed manner, his range of interests, and his gift for expressing himself. Date Masamune had never spoken to Shiro like this. Date Masamune was physically rigid. Even when relaxing, like that day in the bath and at tea afterwards, he stood, sat, and kneeled straight and square. Perhaps it was the Japanese way. Perhaps it was an effect from having known so many battles. Perhaps, Shiro even wondered if the Lord was more relaxed with others and only rigid with him because he was ashamed of him.

Three people paid careful attention to the spectacle of Shiro engaged in such animated conversation with the King of Spain: Hasekura Tsunenaga, Father Sotelo, and Marta Vélez. This latter personage, dressed in black, approached the young Samurai as soon as she found the proper opportunity.

'Do you remember me?' she asked.

Shiro bowed.

'Of course I do, my lady.'

'I knew,' she said, pointing at him with her closed fan, 'from the moment we met that you were different from the rest, and that there would be a profitable future in store for you.'

This woman, he thought, is a trouble-maker, a *Yoku-shi-gaki*. She had all the airs of a flattering temptress, guaranteed to transform whatever business or relation one might engage in with her into pain and trouble.

'I am quite like my other Samurai brothers,' he said. 'And my future, anyone's, is entirely unpredictable, madam.'

She waved his adolescent philosophizing aside.

'Do you recall our first conversation?' she asked.

'Something to do with baths and bathing,' he replied.

'Precisely,' she said. Now she was the flattered one. 'Well, here you are in Madrid. My offer still stands. I have company this evening, but if you were to come by my home tomorrow after sunset, the bath would be all yours to enjoy.'

He bowed again, stalling. Trouble or not, he thought, a bath was a bath.

'And how shall I know how to find it?'

'It's the number Six on the Carrer de San Jerónimo. A twenty-minute walk from here.'

Feeling indisposed, Don Rodrigo left the reception early, and Marta Vélez went with him. As Shiro watched them leave, he was more interested in the physiognomy of the gentleman than the lady's, for it intrigued him to observe the man who had sired Guada. He looked for points of comparison but found few. Grown red-faced and portly from too many years of excessive food and drink, the man bore scant resemblance to his exquisite daughter. The coloring perhaps, Shiro thought, and a certain bearing. Despite his digestive afflictions, the nobleman moved with grace.

Once outside, the couple stood under shelter from what by then was only a drizzle. They were waiting for her carriage to pull up. Across the way, Marta noticed a common-looking young woman with a somber gentleman in humble garb at her side arguing with one of the royal guards. She swore she heard the girl pronounce the word *Shiro*. Marta Vélez asked Don Rodrigo to bear with her a moment while she walked over to sate her curiosity. Deferred to by the guard, Marta soon convinced an initially reluctant Rocío Sánchez that she would be more than happy to ensure that Shiro receive the young woman's note on the following day.

Back in the reception hall, broad shafts of clean light with an amber tint shot through the windows as the rain abated, causing all within to comment. The *Infantas* in residence and their coterie moved outside into a protected garden to breathe the fresh air. The Duke of Lerma was eager to curtail the event as soon as possible, for he had further business to attend to and a romantic assignation with a tutor of his children, a Rabbi's daughter from Toledo. It was to take place at his sumptuous Madrid residence, the Quinta del Prior in the famous *camerín,* lined with paintings. Smitten by her a year earlier, he had obtained a writ of exemption that allowed her to remain in his employ free from persecution.

For the Spaniards in attendance, the novelty of the Japanese Delegation had all but worn off. Made sleepy by the assortment of sweetmeats, ham, and sherry, most were looking to be on their way home for a siesta. The King sensed it and began to make his farewells, moving from group to group. When he came upon Shiro and the Duke of Medina-Sidonia, he asked them to accompany him on the following day to the Pardo Palace, which was hidden within the royal hunting grounds just north of the city. As the King left the hall, the Duke of Lerma assured the Monarch that he would see to it that the Japanese and their Franciscan translator would be properly bid adieu and taken care of for the rest of the evening.

Hasekura Tsunenaga watched as the King of Spain patted Shiro on the back before taking leave, and he had to marvel at the young man's success. He, too, was tired from the strain of being so long in such a foreign land, tired from having to stand like a mummy next to the odorous priest, unable to speak his own mind directly to their hosts. He wished to retire and lie down, alone, and collect his wits. Looking out at the colorful women in the wet garden, he wondered if his father had already been beheaded back in Sendai. He wondered at this strange pantomime he had been coerced into by Date Masamune.

Upon reaching her residence, Marta Vélez put Don Rodrigo to bed and was more than pleased to observe him drift off into a deep sleep that would last until the morning. Left to her own devices, she opened the note the girl had handed her:

Esteemed Shiro—I beg and pray these words reach your eyes, for I believe you were a trusted friend of my husband, Diego Molina, who sailed with you across the world and who was vilely murdered in the olive groves where he worked so tirelessly. I found him bound to a tree and run through by a sword. He was on the verge of death, and his last words to me were that I should tell you it was the Nobleman, the 'knave,' the two of you met in Sanlúcar de Barrameda. Diego was a good man, a decent man. I waited for him for many years to return from his travels, only to find him thus assaulted after only a month of happiness together. I shall never recover nor do I wish to. I who have no connection with power or nobility plead with you to honor him by avenging his death. May God bless you and protect you. Rocío Sánchez de Molina.

Julian, Marta thought to herself, what have you done? And what should I do? Though she knew at once the answer. In the end, the foreigner was someone of impure blood and not one of them, an appealing distraction for sure and perhaps a delicacy to be savored on the following evening, but she would not hand him the note under any circumstances. And on the following morning, she paid a retainer of Don Rodrigo who traveled with him and to whom she had always been generous to take the note and deliver it into the hand of Don Julian.

– XXVI –

In which Shiro makes a powerful friend and a violation is foretold

The Duke of Lerma collected Shiro and the Duke of Medina-Sidonia at dawn, and with an escort of forty men, they galloped into the woods north of Madrid. Having decided, despite the King's infatuation, that the young Japanese man was far beneath him, the Duke of Lerma spent the journey conversing with his fellow nobleman about family matters, court intrigues, and when the Duke of Medina-Sidonia's annulment might be expected from the Vatican.

Shiro did not mind and was content to admire the scenery. The sky had cleared completely, and a semicircle of mountains shone brightly before them, their worn-down peaks covered with gleaming snow. As they entered the royal grounds, herds of deer and wild boars ran about them. The Palace, hidden in the woods, had an exterior with a pinkish hue that contrasted most pleasingly with the greenery surrounding it. The Samurai was enchanted.

As they approached, the King came at them on horseback on a path from the east and joined them, calling out a hearty welcome. A meal was served in the entrance hall. Shiro ate very little and only drank water.

'Seeing as how you have expressed such enthusiasm for our painters, young man, I wanted to show you something very special,' said the King, standing from the table as the meal concluded.

The Duke of Medina-Sidonia gave Shiro a light pat on the back in approbation for the favorable impression he had made.

'A fire swept through here some years ago,' the King continued, 'but the painting I wish to show you was spared, and I have taken it ever since as a good omen.'

They walked through wide hallways lined with portraits and still lifes by Anthonis Mor, his pupil Alonso Sánchez Coello, and the latter's disciple Juan Pantoja de la Cruz. Taking a turn into a windowless room lined with red velvet, the King walked right past Correggio's *Rape of Ganymede*. Shiro, keeping apace with the Monarch and the limping Grandee, could not believe his eyes. The painting depicted the figure of a naked boy-child wrapped in a cloak the color of faded pomegranate who was being lifted off the ground into a Mediterranean blue sky by an enormous bird of prey. An autumnal poplar tree stood to the left, and a startled dog just below was barking at the spectacle, looking up.

They soon arrived at the King's destination, a room that occupied a far corner of the palace. It was a high-ceilinged chamber that faced the open countryside looking north and west. It had simple furniture and two modestly proportioned windows between which hung a large painting some four meters long and two meters high.

'This,' said the King to his guests, 'is my favorite.'

It was a dark landscape portraying, at an indeterminate time of day—twilight perhaps, or early morning—a clearing in the woods. Moving from left to right, a man blows upon a clarion made from

an animal's horn, a man it seems in service to a hunting party behind him and out of sight. Another man, younger and athletically
rendered, with two fine dogs on leashes, is calling out to the unseen
hunting party while pointing at a buck by a stream. The buck is seen
in the background at the far left of the painting, being set upon by
dogs that have been unleashed by yet another colleague. Though
handsome, clean shaven, and well put together, the second youth is
oblivious to the fact that a young woman seated on the ground next
to him, his sister or his sweetheart perhaps, is being spoken to and
more than likely propositioned by a heavily bearded, naked Satyr
facing her, his back to the viewer, his head adorned with a simple
wreath of laurel. But the Satyr is not looking at her directly. He is
looking up toward the very center of the painting that is delineated
by the slender trunk of a tall tree on whose upper branch can be seen
the naked, infantile personage of Eros. This pudgy little god is aiming his bow down toward two other forms that dominate the entire
composition; a naked woman partially covered by a shroud, young,
blond, somewhat corpulent in the fashion of the time and seemingly
asleep, and another Satyr—this one with a more cunning and avaricious appearance than the first. The Satyr is pulling the shroud off
the maiden. But his gaze is not affixed upon her appealing flesh yet,
but rather at the arrow being pointed at him from above. It seems
as if these Satyrs are mainly interested in the figure up in the tree
between them, there to facilitate what will happen next, and it is
as if the hunting party of ordinary mortals around them with their
dogs cannot see them.

'What do you make of it Shiro San?' asked the King.

Aware that to a certain extent he was being evaluated, Shiro took
his time and answered with caution.

'Hunting,' he replied. 'Hunting of various sorts.'

'Very good,' said the King. 'Go on.'

'The three men and their dogs are hunting the deer. The other two men, who look to be shaped like animals from the waist down, are after the women.'

'They are Satyrs, pleasure seekers, sexual predators who are companions of the Greek gods Pan and Dionysus. And what do you make of the little fellow up in the tree?'

'A baby with a bow and arrow. I confess I have no idea. He seems to be aiming the arrow directly at the Satyr next to the naked woman, but the Satyr looks to be unconcerned.'

'What do you know of the Greeks?' asked the King.

'Very little, Your Majesty. In truth, I have only begun to learn something about the Romans, thanks to the patience of the Duke.'

'The Greeks predated the Romans by hundreds of years,' said the King. 'All that is worthy about the Romans comes from the Greeks, and the Greeks had many gods who sometimes would assume human form in order to mate with humans they fancied, or to tease them, help them, torment them.'

'I assume this was a manner in which the Greeks chose to explain their troubles, Your Majesty,' said Shiro. 'Like your own Jesus, who was a god but who became a man for a time. It is a recourse all societies I know of resort to.'

The Monarch stared at Shiro with some amazement, then at the Duke. 'Best to keep this young man clear of my Inquisitors, Alonso."

'Quite, Your Majesty,' answered the Duke with a grin.

'Be that as it may,' said the King, returning his attention to the Samurai. 'In this particular case, this Satyr here is Zeus,' he said, pointing at the Satyr placed in the middle of the composition, 'the king of the gods, known by the name of Jupiter to the Romans, and he is on the verge of possessing this fetching maiden who was called Antiope, a beautiful princess, daughter to a man called Prince

Nykteus. When the Prince later discovered that his daughter was pregnant, she fled from his wrath and set all manner of things into motion.'

'And was the child born?' Shiro asked, looking at the sleeping Antiope.

'Twins were born, Amphion and Zethos.'

'Princes born out of wedlock,' said the Duke nodding toward the Samurai.

'The presence of Eros,' continued the King, 'who the Romans called Amor, from which our own word for love derives, is symbolic. Whoever receives an arrow from his quiver falls in love, becomes inflamed with passion. Rather than depict the actual moment of possession, which would have been vulgar and sinful for Titian, for so the painter was called—he did this painting for my father, and it took him thirty-two years to finish it to his satisfaction—the figure of Eros and his bow is there to inform us as to what is about to happen.'

'I see,' said Shiro. 'I understand. And look at the quiver of arrows. I'd give much for one like it. But surely the presence of the hunters and their dogs and the deer being attacked must be symbolic, as well.'

'I assume they are there for contrast of some sort,' said the King. 'Though in both cases a defenseless creature, the deer in one case, the maiden in the other, hover on the brink of violation.'

– XXVII –

In which a mistress changes her mind

Marta Vélez sent her servants away and prepared the bath herself. She remained beside it as Shiro disrobed and descended into the hot water. Despite his being accustomed to nakedness around the opposite sex back home, something about the intimacy of that evening, the luxurious and foreign setting, the tiles and furnishings, aroused him as he undressed. The beauty of his body combined with his inability to hide his desire convinced the Spanish woman to disrobe as well and join him.

They awakened in her bed the following dawn to the sound of the city's church bells calling the faithful to Lauds. The unexpected tenderness of his attentions throughout the night and the pleasures it gave her had broken through Marta's brittle facade. As the light of day crept under thick curtains, she began to regret what she had done with the note.

Bracing herself for his wrath, she confessed to him her encounter with Rocío Sánchez. She revealed the contents of the note and told him what she had done with it. He listened in silence and remained so afterwards until she pled with him to say something.

'I thank you for telling me,' he said. 'I must go.'

She watched him dress in the faint light of the room. For a moment she feared for her life as he picked up his sword and knife. But all he did was bow to her, and then he was gone.

The few madrileños on the street at that hour stared at him and pointed at him. The air was clear and cold. The guards at the Monasterio de San Francisco where the Samurai were lodged made way for him. By noon he was on his way back south, ostensibly accompanying the Duke of Medina-Sidonia, who was returning to Sevilla and then to his ancestral home. The Duke of Lerma saw them off personally and presented Shiro with two books and a gift from the King. The books were a copy of the Jesuit Roberto Bellarmino's *Doctrina Cristiana* and Fray Luis de Granada's *Libro de la oración*. The gift from the King, toiled on overnight, was an exact replica of the red leather quiver, replete with royal arrows, that Shiro had so admired in Titian's painting.

Three days into their journey, just north of Merida and at the Duke's insistence, they rode for a number of hours through a bitter rainstorm, and that evening the Grandee took ill. Shiro and a local physician broke the fever and nursed him back to health, but owing to his weakened state, the Duke decided to recuperate in the more temperate climate provided at his palace in Sanlúcar, the town of his birth. A letter was dispatched to Rosario asking her to join him there. Despite Shiro's impatience, he remained with the Duke, riding right through Sevilla, and they arrived at Sanlúcar de Barrameda on a clear and mild winter's evening.

The suite assigned to Shiro, one of the finest in the palace, was the same one Julian and Marta Vélez had occupied when he first met them. Since he had made a point of not revealing to the Duke his true motive for returning south, he had no choice but to gratefully accept the suite, though for the three nights he remained there, he slept upon the floor. As soon as Rosario arrived along with a score of additional servants from Medina-Sidonia, Shiro bid them adieu. The Duke thanked him for his aide and company and hoped that the Baptism ceremony of Hasekura Tsunenaga would not prove to be a bore. He made Shiro promise to come visit them again in the spring before the Delegation left for Rome.

Shiro bowed to the both of them, holding back a swell of emotion that took him by surprise and that the couple noted but remained silent about. The young Samurai was fairly certain they would never see one another again. After avenging the death of Diego Molina, he would be a renegade, a wanted man who, under no circumstances, would ever allow himself to be taken alive.

– XXVIII –

In which the gates of hell are opened

The only good fortune Shiro had that evening upon entering the grand house belonging to Julian and Guada was being grabbed at once by two men who prevented him from drawing his sword. Had he been able to attack them, with what would have been a predictable outcome, the other two men who ran into the entrance patio carrying cocked muskets would have fired and killed him. As it was the first two gripped him by either arm, and the second pair aimed their barrels at his heart. Julian appeared on the balcony above and, seconds later, Guada with him. Before descending the stone stairs, he bade her to return to her chamber, but she refused.

Down below he walked over to Shiro. 'I've been waiting for you.'

'You murdered my friend,' said the Samurai. 'You murdered him like a coward. You did not even have the decency to challenge him and hand him a weapon.'

Julian addressed his men. 'The monkey speaks.'

The men laughed, nervously.

'I am a nobleman, you mongrel,' Julian spit back, gathering anger. 'Your "friend" was a common sailor, or something to that effect. Why on earth would I challenge him? It would have been an insult to my family.'

'Leave him be,' called Guada from the balcony.

Her husband turned and screamed at her, 'Go away!'

He removed Shiro's bow and the red leather quiver, tossing them to the tiled floor. He took Shiro's sword and Tanto in hand, admiring them. 'A fine piece of craftsmanship. Too fine for the likes of you. Perhaps you stole them. Sharp, too, I would imagine.'

He took the Tanto and stabbed it an inch into Shiro's left shoulder, drawing blood. The Samurai winced but showed no further distress. Then Julian turned the blade, causing more blood to flow. Sweat broke out on Shiro's forehead. Julian withdrew the blade.

'Tougher than your friend. I'll say that for you. He screamed like a pig.'

Guada screamed when she saw her husband stab the Samurai, and she called out again. 'You mustn't kill him. I shall never forgive you if you do. I will denounce you, and the Duke will hunt you down.'

Julian turned and looked up at her with pure hatred.

'Will you not obey me, woman? Return to your chambers.'

'I will not,' she cried.

He turned back to his men.

'Put him on the ground, and you two, break his hands with the butts of your muskets.'

The men did as they were told, and this time Shiro cried out in agony, in shock from the pain and from the humiliation. Guada began to scream and come down the stairs. Julian turned to one of the men holding a musket.

'Seize her. Do not let her down here.'

Then he got on his knees near Shiro, whose hands were already beginning to swell.

'So much for the warrior,' Julian said. 'But there's just one more thing.'

Still holding the Tanto, he separated Shiro's sixth finger out and leaned the blade down upon it. The pain already flooding the Samurai's system was such that he barely felt it.

'I'll spare your life,' Julian said, 'but I will not permit a freak in my home.'

He got back on his feet and addressed the three remaining men. 'Throw him into the street and lock the doors.'

They dragged the Samurai over the pink-and-white tiles that were streaked with blood, and over the wooden lip of the massive front door, tossing him onto the manure-strewn cobblestones in front of the mansion. Then they shut and bolted the doors.

Julian dropped the Tanto and tossed the severed finger away. Nervous, frightened, exhilarated, and incensed, he herded the man with Guada back up the stairs. He told all four of the men to leave them alone and to tell the servants the same thing. He pushed Guada into a sitting room and slammed the door. He began to hit her and tear off her clothing, ignoring her screams and fists and her repeated cries of 'Murderer.' And then he raped her.

When he was done and rolled off of her, she ceased to struggle. She looked away, breathing furiously. No matter how much he yelled at her to look at him, she would not do it. He finally left her naked and bruised on the wrinkled rug. The remorse he felt afterward, and the shaking that invaded his system, was nevertheless infused with animal satisfaction. And though Guada, from then on, would refuse to sleep with him or to be alone with him in the same room ever again, in a month's time she found herself with child.

– XXIX –

In which the Guadalquivir flows to the sea

He dragged himself for a kilometer and found a stable and hid there next to a mule until the middle of the night. He lost consciousness from the pain, and then, upon regaining it, he would shake from the shock to his system. When all was quiet, he forced himself onto his feet, his mangled hands hanging at his sides. He walked to the bridge that spanned the Guadalquivir, the one the Japanese Delegation had crossed so triumphantly a month earlier. Seeing no one about and unable to commit Seppuku, he made his way across to the middle and cast himself over the edge.

He hoped to drown. But no matter how far he dove or how much water he attempted to swallow, his body kept struggling to the surface. The current swept him west, and then south, and by the time the sun rose, he staggered out of the water and collapsed upon a muddy bank next to the village of Coria del Río.

A young woman found him and alerted her father, a sturgeon fisherman who called for the local priest. The priest was an elderly man believed to be a *curandero* blessed with healing powers. But when he saw the Samurai, he pronounced him to be a river devil come to infect the village with sin. When Shiro managed to say, 'Soy Catolico,' it only agitated the cleric further, and as he scurried back to his church, he counseled the fisherman to throw 'the beast' back into the river.

Then the fisherman sent his daughter to fetch *El Camborio*, a Gypsy who was a shrewder sort well schooled in the properties of plants and herbs. He saw in Shiro a kindred spirit, a fellow outcast, and also recognized a figure of some distinction from whom he might receive a handsome compensation.

El Camborio smoked a small pipe held upside down and was the man all of the villagers went to when a goat or sheep required slaughtering. A narrow, entirely decorative cane hung off his right wrist, and no matter how tattered his cloak or trousers, his shirts were always clean. He carried himself like a dandy under a wide-brimmed hat. He smelled of garlic and thyme and kept a family back in the hills, where he often roamed during the early mornings gathering sprigs and blossoms. He cleaned and sewed up the wound in Shiro's shoulder and set the bones of Shiro's hands.

The fisherman was called Francisco, and he took the Samurai in to recover with his wife and family. They set aside a corner of their small house for him. It was close to the river and made from bricks of mud and straw that were whitewashed. For many days, El Camborio came to massage Shiro's hands with Manzanilla, olive oil, and caviar. He insisted the latter ingredient was essential for proper healing but most in the village believed it was only an excuse to savor the precious roe reaped by the fishermen.

The pain in Shiro's hands was renewed with each day's treatments, but he did improve. Seven of his now ten fingers went numb. He asked the Gypsy if he might ever wield a sword again, and the man shook his head.

'You will be fortunate if someday you can hold yourself again when urinating, or use those little twigs of yours for eating.'

When he was well enough, Shiro moved into a hut of his own by the riverbank. Many of the villagers contributed to his want of food and drink. Some had heard of the Delegation that had come to Spain from far away and that had passed nearby on its way north to Sevilla months earlier. They were amazed to hear the foreigner speaking Spanish and felt remorse upon hearing the explanation he gave for his sorry state—one that omitted the names of his allies and enemies.

Two months passed. The Baptism ceremony for Hasekura Tsunenaga was long gone. Shiro wondered how they had appraised his absence. One day he found he was able to hold a cup to drink from and that he was able to tie his robe unaided. Though still numb, many of his damaged fingers now thrummed within, an uncomfortable sensation that came and went. On the evening of the spring equinox, Francisco came to speak with him.

'My daughter Piedad has taken a fancy to you. If it is true that you have taken the sacraments, I would be inclined to please her by telling her you would agree to marry. We know you have no funds and we know you can no longer work as normal men do, but you could make yourself useful and be safe here and give us grandchildren.'

From the moment she had found him, looking more like a water-logged, half-dead reptile than a man, Piedad had admired him and dreamed about him. And she had fed him during the first weeks of his recovery. When he moved into his own hut, they took walks together along paths that followed the river. She took to joining him under his blanket late at night.

'You honor me, too much,' Shiro replied. 'I fear I am not the right person to become her husband. The kindness she has shown me, that you and the others have bestowed upon me, shall never be forgotten until the day I die. But my own people, the Lord I serve, my own mother await my return. And there is still revenge in my heart for what has been done to me. The code I follow demands that I attend to it.'

Francisco looked out at the flattened earth in front of the hut, at four chickens pecking about its perimeter, at the reeds and the river. Spring was well advanced, and the trees were lush with leaves and blossoms that made a whispering noise in the afternoon breeze.

'You would do well to stay, young man. It was fate that brought you here to us, fate that Piedad discovered you. You are lucky to be alive. I urge you to reconsider, to abandon your need for revenge, and to embrace instead this gentle place, this simple, good life, and to accept my love-besotted daughter to be your wife.'

The sturgeon fishermen built small rafts used to connect a series of nets together under the water into which the prehistoric fish swam laden with their tasty little eggs. Shiro took one of the rafts that had been put aside for repair and left the village that night. He shoved off into the middle of the current and used a fallen branch he could barely grasp to steer with.

By dawn he had reached the hamlet of La Señuela, where he hid the raft and ate bits of bread he'd wrapped in a cloth. As the daylight hours went by, he slept or stared at his sorry hands and performed all of the exercises El Camborio had taught him. When Venus appeared, the evening star, he pushed back out into the river, and by the following dawn he arrived in Sanlúcar de Barrameda.

The water there was no longer fresh, but salty from the sea. It smelled of clean brine and ocean, and it was colder and deeper even as the air he breathed was warm. The shore he set foot on was made from sand rather than mud, and walking toward the town as the sun came up, he reached the dock where their ship had been moored, where he'd spent his first night in Spain. The ship was no longer there, and the dock was empty. Above in the sky that had lightened into a tender blush of pale blue, the moon was still visible and in that light could be seen as a fading sphere.

– XXX –

In which a mother is lost and another gained

On the night she and Shiro were assaulted, Guada fled her house by way of the servant's entrance and walked the streets alone until she reached the palacete of her parents. Both were in residence and appalled by the bruises about her face and the violent tale she related. Rodrigo, somewhat unconvincingly, for neither woman paid him much mind when he said it, promised to give Julian 'a thorough thrashing he'll never forget.'

But by the following morning their tone had cooled. Rodrigo left the house early to visit an estate, and Doña Inmaculada came to Guada's bedroom when her daughter was taking breakfast.

'How long do you plan on staying here?' the mother asked.

'For as long as I have to,' said Guada. 'Until we can get Julian to leave my house.'

'It is his house.'

'But you gave it to me.'

'We gave it to the both of you, but it is, of course, registered in his name. It was part of your dowry and the least we could do in exchange for the lands that came to us from his family.'

'What are you telling me, mother?'

'That perhaps you should give him some time to calm down and apologize.'

Tears came into the girl's bloodshot eyes.

'He beat me and raped me. Apparently, he has killed a man in cold blood and had another brutally assaulted before my eyes. What are you saying?'

Guada began to cry. Inmaculada sat on the bed near her daughter but made no move to comfort her.

'Do you remember the conversation we had, in Carmona, before you were married?' Doña Inmaculada asked.

'What of it?'

'You asked me whether your father had been gentle with me, ever. And I explained to you how we came to no longer share a bed.'

Inmaculada paused for a moment, taking a fold of Guada's coverlet between her ring and index fingers, recalling its provenance, from her own mother's dowry.

'There was a time when my life with your father sometimes resembled what you went through yesterday. Men are beasts, my dear. Look at what was done to our savior. Study the Stations of the Cross. And yet you and your brother were born and prospered. Your father and I still live under the same roof. We have learned, over time, to be civil with each other, even to appreciate each other.'

Guada dried her tears with a large linen napkin.

'My father and Julian share the same whore.'

'And what does that tell you?' Inmaculada asked.

Guada looked away, feeling betrayed and alone, a stranger in her own home. She saw what they were up to. She looked back at Doña Inmaculada, swearing to herself that she would do all in her power

to never acquiesce and end up like her mother. But all she said was
'Very well mother.'

'Very well what?'

'I shall think on what you have said.'

After breakfast and her toilette, after examining her face in a mirror
and reliving once again all that had befallen her, she sent a note to
her aunt Soledad, who responded immediately. By early that afternoon, she had moved once again.

'Your mother is a sufferer,' Doña Soledad said. 'I am not.'

They were seated together in the same light-filled chamber where
the older woman had received the Duke.

'I withstood a tempest,' she added. 'But not for long.'

'What can I do?' Guada asked.

'Very little,' her aunt replied. 'That is to say, there are some fun-
damental things you cannot change. As women, we have scant recourse. The house is his. You cannot throw him out, though perhaps
he will tire of Sevilla and leave of his own accord. I remained in mine
and bolted my suites to my husband, and he continued to carry on in
his own part of the house like a drunken fool until he died from it.'

'I cannot go back there,' Guada said. 'I cannot be alone with
him, anywhere, ever again, nor do I wish to set eyes upon him, ever
again.'

'Then you shall stay with me,' Soledad said, taking her niece's
hand. 'For as long as you wish. And when I die, this house shall be
yours. And he will never be admitted here or to any of my properties
that will all be yours someday, as well.'

Guada began to cry again, this time from gratitude, and she put
her arms about her aunt, who in turn held the girl close and kissed
the top of her head.

'I hope you can pardon me for what I am about to say,' her aunt
went on, speaking gently but with a tremor of anger in her voice.
'But it is my view that your parents are greedy, needlessly so because
they are extremely wealthy. The estates that have been added to their
ledgers thanks to your marriage mean, I fear, as much to them as
your own happiness. I do not understand it. It is as if Inmaculada
wishes you to have the life she has had.'

'I won't,' Guada said.

Soledad looked at her intently, tears coming into her eyes, as well.

'No, you won't. I can see that. And, you know, despite their avarice, ours is the better family by many gradations, something those
in power appreciate.'

'For whatever good that does me,' Guada said.

'It means that over time, as word goes around, Julian's star shall
dim, more and more, and when you take a lover, the King shall approve.'

'A lover.'

'Alonso informed me you had a suitor, though I'm afraid he shall
never do.'

'A suitor?'

'A young man from Japan, one who speaks Spanish and who, according to the Duke, saved his life.'

Guada lowered her head and smiled to think the Duke had said
such a thing to her aunt, but then the smile turned into a look of
distress.

'What is it, Guada?'

'The man you speak of is the one Julian had beaten so badly. They
stabbed him and broke his hands and threw him into the street.'

'No.'

'Yes.'

'Perhaps then it was jealousy on Julian's part.'

173

'No. Julian knows nothing, not that there was anything to know. Shiro—for that is how the foreigner is called—came to avenge the death of a friend he accused Julian of murdering.'

Soledad continued to hold her niece, listening to all she said, and as she listened, she gave silent thanks for her advanced years, for she remembered how painful it was to be young.

– XXXI –

In which Hasekura Tsunenaga takes a breath

Born Hasekura Rokuemon Tsunenaga in the Sendai Domain in 1571, he was baptized by the barbarians Don Francisco Felipe Faxicura, the surname being their best approximation of his real name. Since the day of the ceremony, he attended mass each morning and prayed each afternoon with Father Sotelo along with six other Samurais who'd taken their conversion to heart.

But on the day that Shiro returned to Sanlúcar by the river raft, Hasekura was standing in his room in the Monasterio de San Francisco, staring out through a narrow window at fertile green plains rolling westward. He was feeling weary and homesick once again. The Christian imagery he had been subjected to day after day had worn him down: the whippings and the flayings, the bleeding victim nailed to a cross. The myriad restrictions insisted upon by his new faith confounded him. And for however intently he mouthed the prayers, shutting his eyes tight, nothing seemed to come of it.

What was he doing so far from home? In the core of his being he sensed it was time to move on, to get the rest of the journey over with. To be back at sea, even though it meant a voyage to Rome that was farther still from the land of his ancestors, would at least mean he'd be that much closer to completing the mission, that much closer to being able to set sail for Sendai.

Everything went so slowly in this country, the layers of bureaucracy, the finding and provisioning of a ship, the letters and permissions sent back and forth. And what, he wondered, had become of Shiro? Had the boy gone native? Or perhaps he had gotten himself into trouble, or fallen ill, or worse. And if so, how might Date Masamune react? Might the powerful Daimyo hold him responsible? He determined to make an effort to look for the young Samurai, or at least to seem to.

Rather than attend yet another foul meal with the others, one that would be prefaced by yet more prayers, he decided instead to take a walk. He wished to leave the dark, musty palace for the fresh, clean air blowing down from the nearby mountains. Spring had come and taken over the landscape, permeating the city and the surrounding plains with verdancy and blossoms. Gathering his gear and descending to the front hall, he stated his intentions to the priests and the guards and moved quickly into the narrow streets before someone might hail him, attach themself to him, slow him down.

In half an hour's time, striding east, he'd passed the San Jerónimo El Real Church and entered a placid, wooded park where beggars abounded, where couples walked together, chaperones in tow, where families congregated on the grass to take their midday meal. He came to a stream that ran through a glen. The earth, refreshed and invigorated, smelled of pine and rosemary, the air carried a delicate scent of lilac and honeysuckle. Though he was stared and pointed at, the passersby always greeted him with respect. His somber mood lifted, and he was forced to admit that despite their gloomy religion, these Spaniards had something commendable about them—a pride in their gait, a ready smile, a courteousness that rivaled his own.

He slaked his thirst in the stream and found a sunlit expanse of grass nearby and lay down upon his back. Above he looked at the bluest of skies and at sculpted clusters of the upper branches of three Mediterranean pines. He closed his eyes and felt the sun upon his lids, seeing red through them. He inhaled the air, listening to the stream and to children playing in the distance. His father and older brother would be dead by now, his disgraced mother bitter and inconsolable. Perhaps it was not all that bad to be there in the sunlight on the other side of the Earth.

– XXXII –

In which the Admiral bids the world adieu

Rosario was in her first trimester and showing. 'He fell ill on the evening the annulment arrived from Rome. We were in bed after celebrating. He had had too much to drink. Suddenly the blood drained from his face, and he began to moan and vomit. Eventually he calmed down and fell asleep. I cleaned him and cleaned the floor and let him be. In the morning I found him in tears, half of his body, his left side, paralyzed, half of his face drooping. He was unable to speak. The doctors came and bled him and prepared all manner of herbs and potions. But nothing helped. After a week or so he improved and insisted we marry immediately in case he suffered a relapse. The priest came to the bedroom along with the mayor who served as our witness. For the next few days he seemed to get better still, but then he had another attack."

'May I see him?' Shiro asked.

'Of course,' she said. 'He'll be so pleased you've returned.'

'Might there be some garments I could borrow?'

'Certainly.'

'Does his son know? Does the King know?'

'Juan Manuel was here last week and left distraught. As for the King, I have no idea.'

'Was he kind to you?'

'Who?'

'Juan Manuel.'

'He was civil. Though when he saw I was carrying his father's child he seemed irritated.'

'How could he leave his father's side?'

The Duke's bedroom in Sanlúcar commanded an impressive view of the beach and the swirling tides of the delta. The water was green that morning where the river met the sea, and there was a sandbar showing and the sun sparkled on the surface of the water all the way across to the wetlands. A suit of armor stood in a corner next to the model of a Spanish galleon. The bed was high and canopied and enclosed with heavy velvet curtains dyed a deep burgundy.

Shiro came in behind Rosario. The Samurai had changed from what remained of his ragged robe and trousers into Christian garb. He kept his hands behind him. The Duke was awake, and when he recognized the Samurai he made a grunting noise laced with satisfaction. Shiro smiled and tried to conceal his alarm, for his friend looked much older and frail. The Duke motioned for Rosario to hand him a pen and paper. He wrote something and handed it to Shiro. It read—where are your clothes?

The Samurai smiled and said, 'I've had an adventure and lost them along the way.'

The Duke attempted to smile back, but with his good eye he studied the young man carefully, taking in his rough-hewn countenance. Then he reached out with his right hand, forcing Shiro to reveal his own. He hoped the Duke would not notice the damage done to it, but the hope was in vain. The grandee examined the mangled fingers that, though recovered with some movement, still bore scars and presented an appendage difficult to contemplate. He then motioned to see the other hand, and Shiro showed it to him. Rosario left them alone.

For a long time afterwards, Shiro would torture himself with the thought that the anger his tale elicited from the Duke had been the cause of the nobleman's final stroke. Later that night, after Shiro and Rosario finished the evening meal, they went to the master bedroom to say goodnight and found the Grandee alive but unresponsive. Three days later he was dead.

Often during the last five years, the Duke had wondered how it might be, how it might come. It came during the night and woke him up. It was as if something inside had given out, opened, and loosened, and his life was suddenly flowing away. It did not hurt. But as he realized the gravity of it, the absolute finality of it, his fragile heart fluttered with fear. He tried to hold on at first, to keep his eye on the moon out the window, as if to grab onto a branch or some exposed root protruding from the riverbank. But his vision darkened, and the branch broke. The root proved too slippery. He was too frightened to pray. As his spirit dimmed and the world went on oblivious to his drama, he searched out memories in the hope one might assuage him. But instead, the memories that came at him seemingly did so of their own accord, rose up from god knows where within his dimming brain.

His mother's hand holding his as they walked along the beach on a sunlit morning and the sound of her voice. The horses being driven off his ship into the Irish Sea, but now he was in the water with them and the ship moved on. A day as a lad when he'd gotten lost in the Sierra Morena and fallen asleep under a tree and then woke at dawn on damp earth hearing birds, new to the world.

– XXXIII –

In which a verdugo raises welts and Guada writes a letter

Shiro was not prepared to face some of those who would come for the funeral, and he was concerned that Julian might be among them. He decided to leave. Rosario offered him the palace in Medina-Sidonia and he accepted.

On his last night in Sanlúcar, he heard sounds of flagellation coming from Rosario's chamber. Pushing past a maid guarding her mistress's door, he knocked and then entered. Rosario was naked from the waist up and whipping herself with a stay, a *verdugo* she'd removed from her hoopskirt. Her back was a crisscross of welts. Tears streamed down her cheeks and breasts. He bade her to cease, but she ignored him until he came up to her and grabbed as best he could the wrist of the hand holding the verdugo. She stared at his hand and renewed her sobs. He gave her a cloak with which to cover herself and held her during that night until the sobbing stopped and she fell asleep. He was gone the following morning.

Guada, Doña Inmaculada, and Soledad Medina attended the funeral. At Guada's insistence, Julian did not. When the burial concluded, Rosario told Guada that Shiro had been there only days before. Guada walked out alone on the terrace overlooking the estuary. She sat on a stone bench and wrote to the Samurai. Doña Soledad, who had wandered up to the master bedroom, looked down at her niece from the window and contemplated the girl's youth and the clean beach beyond still there even though the Duke was gone. He had taken her into the bed behind her, the bed he had died in. They had lain there together still young and content, at least for a while, when the thought of a day like this had been the furthest thing from their minds.

– XXXIII –

In which words are exchanged

Shiro,

Rosario has told me of your state and whereabouts and why it was you came back to Sevilla. She has treated my mother and me more graciously than we deserve. Her untimely widowhood weighs upon us.

I have no words to describe the shock and pain, the anger and despair I felt and feel for what happened to you. But I rejoice to learn you have survived and that you have made some recovery.

If you decide to tear this letter into pieces, I will understand. But if you find room in your heart to answer me, by all means send word in care of my aunt, in Sevilla, Doña Soledad Pérez Medina de la Cerda, in whose home I now reside. Since that horrible evening, I have refused to see my husband, and I shall never do so again.

Yours in Christ, Guada

Doña Guada,

This is the first letter I have ever written in any language. Since my hands have yet to heal properly, a gentleman here still in the late Duke's employ has kindly offered to transcribe it for me.

I know that Don Alonso would have been touched that you and your mother made the journey to Sanlúcar for his interment. I am sorry I was not there. Please know the rancor I sustain against the man you married is exclusive to him. Even in the midst of what occurred that evening, I did hear your cries against it. I have no quarrel with you and only hope for your happiness. I confess I am relieved to read you have separated from him.

I am not ready to face you, or anyone. Had I been defeated with less grievous wounds, I would have ended my life as befits the warrior class to which I belong. There are times even now when I consider it. But something drives me to remain alive, to finish what honor demanded of me that night.

***

Shiro,

I write this now from Sevilla, with gratitude for your kind words I fear I do not merit. Though I did protest what happened to you that night, and paid dearly for it afterwards, it happened in my home. And though I am not Julian, I chose to marry him. It means I cannot trust myself, and thus anyone, anymore. I feel as if I no longer know anything with any certainty.

Yours in Christ, Guada

Guada,

An uncle of mine who was always kind to me tortured a Christian missionary to death. Beasts in the forest lick and suckle their young and then kill their prey with ferocity. You are grateful and kind to me, and yet you saw me behead a man in front of you. Who can explain such things? In your letter you mention a price you paid for my misfortune. If it is not too painful, please tell me what it was.

**

Shiro,

Had you not befriended your sailor friend, Julian would not have come to murder him, and if he had not murdered him, you would not have come seeking revenge. Your hands would still be as they were, and I would not have been forcibly attacked and left bruised on the floor filled with Julian's seed that has taken root within my womb. Such is fate. I am so ashamed.

Yours in Christ, Guada

**

Guada,

You will have to excuse this perhaps illegible scrawl. But given the content of your last letter I feel I must answer it myself in my own hand without an intermediary.

Where does the chain of fate begin? With my own conception and birth? With yours? With Father Sotelo, who brought Diego Molina and me together? With Julian's decision to murder Diego in a cowardly act of erroneous revenge? With your marriage? With my lack of care in defending myself that night? All these factors and many more brought me to your home that evening. But Julian's act of brutality against you was not fated. Nothing that happened that night forced him to do such a thing. He chose to do it. Regardless, I look at my hands and I think of the child growing within you and I curse "the fates" for having brought me into your life.

But I must also confess that meeting you has changed me. Of all the Samurai who could have been chosen to deliver Hasekura Tsunenaga's gift to the Duke, it was I because I speak your language. And there you were at this finca in Medina-Sidonia, where I sit once again. This too must figure into the concept of fate.

I traveled the same route to return here, rested by the same stream, came upon the house on the hill at the same hour, but with so much changed in so short a time. The Duke dead and buried, my hands destroyed, my weapons taken from me, and you, who once upon a time had been so close, far away and wounded.

***

Shiro,

Forgive my petulance. I had no intention of accusing you for what happened to me. I have only myself to blame. I knew of Julian's involvement with Marta Vélez before we married. I committed the sin of pride by believing he would do as promised once our union was sanctified. I was warned by my family and chose to ignore them. There is nothing left to say on the matter, so please let us not revisit it.

As for how one regards fate, I can only rely upon my faith. One is put on Earth as a test to determine whether one's soul deserves eternal life in heaven, or eternal damnation. And since Adam deigned to accept Eve's apple plucked from the Forbidden Tree of Wisdom, we have been endowed with free will. On the other hand, God is all-seeing and thereby knows the course each one of us shall take, and looked at from that place our lives indeed are predetermined. In either case, you are not at fault.

You write that meeting me changed you. I can only pray it has been for the better. But I am ignorant of any influence I may have had upon you.

***

Guada,

Too eager to impress the Duke with my sword on the day I made his acquaintance, I sliced a guard's weapon in half and then followed the arc of its flight through the air. As the sharpened shard descended, I saw you emerge from the chapel with Rosario. You were all in white, your golden hair tied in a braid with ribbons of pale-green silk. You wore gloves and carried your prayer book. I had never seen anything so beautiful. I was fearful the shard might come to harm you. When we walked together that night by the sea on the ancient streets of Baelo Claudia, I was fearful I might utter something foolish or unforgiveable. I kept imagining you dressed in a kimono of the sort the wealthy damsels of Edo wear, and the thought made me dizzy.

Did these emotions change me? In your eyes perhaps they may sound paltry. Many years ago when Father Sotelo gave me instruction in the Christian catechism, he often said that "we are creatures of habit." And

I must cede him that point. Upon arriving here I substituted one Lord for another, the Duke for Date Masamune, putting myself at his service, even feeling a similar strength of fealty and devotion. It is, it seems, what I do. But when you appeared I felt an inner expansion, a fragmentation of my discipline I find hard to describe. I can only say that knowing you has revealed paths of autonomy I had never before considered.

***

Shiro,

You flatter me. No matter how enslaved you may feel to habit, to fealty and service, at least you are a man. Your horizons far surpass any that I, as a woman, even as a privileged woman, will ever get to see. No one in my family, now that the Duke is gone, will prosecute for an annulment of my most unfortunate marriage, especially now that I carry the fiend's child.

My aunt encourages me to take a lover, to follow in the footsteps of our illustrious Marta Vélez . She assures me that my wealth and social rank will protect me from slander. But I am still young. To pass from a virginal blushing bride to a hardened mistress in the blink of an eye is not how I envisioned my life. And yet, unlike you, I have little choice in the matter.

So use your inner expansion well, and for whatever small part I may have played in its appearance I give thanks to God. And I pray to Mary for guidance through my troubles. Were it not for the fact that my brother is already enclosed within a monastery, I would be at the gates of a nunnery in a trice, but it would break the hearts of my parents and my aunt.

***

Guada,

My mother took a lover and enjoyed it while it lasted, and here I am as a result of it. You must look to your happiness. And I beg of you to cease referring to your unborn child as the issue of a fiend. The fiendishness of Julian is there for all to see. But your child is innocent and deserves a fresh start.

Rosario arrived from Sanlúcar yesterday along with the rest of the Duke's household. She wishes to give birth, now in two month's time, here where her mother lives. She also brings word from Madrid. After a memorial service that was held in the Alcázar for the Duke, the King kindly asked after me. Hasekura Tsunenaga pleaded ignorance of my whereabouts, and the King sent a letter to Rosario, who solved the riddle. I am relieved to say she made no mention of my physical state nor of the circumstances that brought it about.

The Delegation is to leave for Rome in less than a month's time, and I debate with myself about whether I should join them. I have been remiss of late in my mission to be the eyes and ears of my Lord in Sendai. But I am still a poor sight and am deprived of my weapons and clothing, and I can barely lift a sword. I fear I might prove to be an embarrassment to my fellow warriors. I spent this morning in meditation within the chapel and then walked up into the hills where the Duke and I used to ride together. I wonder if you and I shall ever see each other again.

– XXXIV –

In which Shiro sets forth once again and peace is made

Sometimes at night Rosario would massage Shiro's hands with olive oil and chamomile, and on one evening, holding one of his hands in both of hers, they kissed. They took walks together in the gardens. They told their own stories and retold stories about the Duke. They shared their meals and talked about Guada and Julian and Marta Vélez and Guada's parents and Soledad Medina, the woman who, once upon a time, had been the love of the Duke's life. They talked about the babies to be born. Shiro's feelings for Guada were clear to the both of them. 'I do not seek to wrest a heart I know to be already taken,' Rosario said to him. 'But you and I are alone for now.'

At night they took comfort in each other until one afternoon four Royal horsemen and four mounted Samurai arrived from Madrid. The Royal guard carried a letter to Shiro from the King. The Samurai handed him a short scroll penned by Hasekura Tsunenaga. Both missives contained the same message, wishing him well and encouraging him to leave Medina-Sidonia with the riders who would escort him to Almería, from where they would sail to Barcelona, where a ship was being prepared for the journey to Rome.

He left a letter for Guada with Rosario to send on to Sevilla, and they slept for a final time in the Duke's bed. The following dawn he kissed Rosario's bare swollen abdomen, dressed, and rode off. To be in one place and grow familiar with a house, its rooms and gardens and the hills above, to be, to exist somewhere specific and then to leave it behind never ceased to impress him. He rode off with his escort on a horse Rosario gave to him, leaning forward in his saddle, doing his best to not look back.

The nine men passed a night in Antequera as guests of Pedro Espinosa and another in Granada with the Pisa de Osorio family, where, touring the Alhambra, Shiro realized how grand the Moorish Era had been in Spain.

From there they rode south to Lanjarón and took the waters and followed the course of the Guadalfeo River until it emptied into the sea outside the port of Motril. Following the beach eastward, they reached Almería two days later.

Shiro was engrossed by the journey, the pine forests they traversed up in the lower Alpujarras, the rolling hills of olive trees for as far as the eye could see, the sweet-scented fig trees growing along the river banks, the coastal plains rife with sugar cane, and then as they reached their destination, the sparse low hills back from the sea that turned into desert.

Sailing north along the eastern coast of Spain, he commiserated with his Samurai brethren, nine of whom were from Sendai and who had known him since he was a young boy. When the King's guards queried him about his injuries, he claimed he'd fallen from a horse and had his hands run over by the wheel of a passing carriage. Upon docking in Barcelona, the group proceeded directly to the ship that would take them to Italy.

Two hours after weighing anchor, Father Sotelo sought him out. The priest had put on weight and acquired a more prosperous look during the extended stay in Madrid. Shiro wondered if the cleric still had the necessary fervor to return to Japan.

'I gave thanks to God upon learning you were still with us here upon the Earth,' said the priest, clutching a large wooden crucifix that hung about his neck.

'Father,' Shiro said, bowing.

'Is it true you have received a letter from the King?'

'Yes.'

'As I said to you in Aranjuez, you will be most helpful to us, Shiro-San.'

The Samurai decided to say nothing, opting instead to bow once again. It was then that he saw Hasekura Tsunenaga appear on the aftcastle. They nodded to each other.

'You will have to excuse me, father. I must speak with the Ambassador.'

'*Vaya con Dios*,' said the friar, making the sign of the cross in the air in front of Shiro's face.

Shiro mounted the stairs and bowed to Hasekura and to the Christian captain at the helm. Hasekura took him aside to the balustrade at the very end of the vessel. The skies were low with clouds, and the sea was gray and thick. The two of them stood in silence for a moment contemplating the frothy wake stretching back to the west.

'I owe you an apology, Shiro-San,' said Hasekura.

'And I one to you,' Shiro replied, 'for disappearing.'

Hasekura brushed the offense away.

'You were correct,' he said, 'from the very beginning Shiro-San, when you complained to me about the intermingling between ourselves and the barbarians. I suspect we have committed a blunder. I will of course continue to do all I must to achieve success, but I've grown weary of them and miss the homeland.'

Shiro could tell the man was speaking in confidence and sensed there was no trickery behind the words.

'I may have been correct back then, Hasekura-San, but look at what I have done since, associating with the Christians more than anyone.'

'Precisely, Shiro-San. And see what it has brought you. From the moment you shook the hand of that sailor, you condemned your own hands to ruin.'

'That may be so, Hasekura-San, but in truth I do not regret it. He was a good man, and many of the barbarians I have befriended are good men, too.'

'I do not deny it. I only say we are too different from them, or I am. The distances are too great. The chasm between our beliefs and theirs too vast.'

'I am surprised to hear you say these things, Hasekura-San.'

'I have thought long and hard about it. I believe that over time you shall come to see it, too. I have treated you improperly, Shiro-San. I would like for us to be friends. You have talents I do not possess. And it is true you carry the blood of Date Masamune and Katakura Kojuro. But you still have the impetuousness of youth. Let us try and work together. I have tired of the priest, but I dare not dismiss him. I no longer trust him. He has become inebriated with power and with the entrées his association with us have gained for him in this part of the world. I wish for you to be present when we speak with this Pope, to keep the translations clear for me.'

Shiro bowed.

'It will be an honor.'

'I will give you one of my swords,' Hasekura continued, 'and see you have some proper raiment.'

Shiro looked out at the water and remembered his disgrace.

'I can barely grip a sword, Hasekura-San.'

'But you will again.'

– XXXV –

In which there is trouble at home with great consequences

Tokugawa Ieyasu was the Shogun of Japan. Known for his astuteness on and off the battlefield, he also cultivated a keen interest in the world outside the Kingdom. He had long tolerated foreign visitors in exchange for the intellectual stimulation their presence provoked.

The Portuguese and the Spanish were the first to catch his attention, and he permitted their proselytizing out of pure curiosity. He was amused at first to see how little progress the Catholics made until one of their leaders, a Jesuit, Alessandro Valignano, who arrived in 1579, realized that in order to make more headway, the order would have to adopt Japanese customs: their manner of dress, their shunning of meat, bathing, not eating with their fingers. Tokugawa Ieyasu marveled at how this small, superficial stratagem bore fruit, converting thousands of his subjects.

He was further intrigued to see, when a moribund, undernourished crew of English merchants washed up on his shores in 1600 aboard a Dutch ship, how vociferously the Jesuits, despite their Christian values, wished to have the half-drowned men put to death.

He granted an audience to the most articulate among the Englishmen, one William Adams, and discovered that, contrary to what the Jesuits had been telling him for years, the European nations were divided into different sects of Christianity that were often at each other's throats. What impressed him more was the discovery that William Adams, a man of exceptional charm, possessed great knowledge in the arts of navigation, something of practical and tactical use. The man's globes and charts, his maps and compasses, his astronomical explanations based on geometry, proved more engrossing than the Jesuits harping on about immaculate conceptions.

Subsequent to Adams's success with the Shogun, the Catholics saw their influence wane. They made themselves even more of a nuisance by escalating their demands, a disastrous ploy that only alienated the Shogun further. While they insisted on their exceptionalism, Adams seemed to understand and appreciate the Japanese way of life. He had no religion to sell. His only interests were trade and science. The Catholic position eroded further still when in 1611 a Spanish Admiral appeared in court, one Sebastián Vizcaíno, who refused to bow down before the Shogun and his son, on the grounds that his own sovereign, Philip the Third, ruled an empire a hundred times grander than Japan's.

William Adams went on to become a trusted counselor of the Shogun and to the Shogun's son afterwards and was granted the rank of Samurai. He took a Japanese wife and had children and gave instruction to Japanese shipbuilders as to how to improve their ocean-faring vessels. He tutored Shiro and taught him English. And when the Shogun desired to rid himself of Sebastián Vizcaíno, Adams supervised the construction of the Date Maru that took the dour conquistador back home along with Hasekura Tsunenaga and the Delegation organized at the Shogun's request by Date Masamune.

On the very day that Hasekura Tsunenaga's baptism took place in Spain, the Shogun learned of a flagrant betrayal in his own court. A local Lord converted to Catholicism was looking to increase the size of his fiefdom. The method he chose was to appeal in secret to one of the Shogun's councilors who had also become a Catholic. When the Shogun was appraised of the affair and realized that the religious bond between the two men superseded their traditional loyalties, he lost all patience with the sect. The councilor was hacked to pieces and the defiant Lord driven into exile.

By this time, there were over 300,000 converts in the realm and 116 missionaries serving them. The Shogun was told that many of the missionaries were imploring their faithful to heed the priests more than the Shogun's representatives. He issued an edict—much as Philip the Third had done in 1609 when he drove the Moors out of Spain—ordering all Catholics to leave the country. Those who remained were compelled to convert to one of the Buddhist sects or suffer execution.

Around the time that Hasekura Tsunenaga and the Delegation prepared to sail from Spain to Rome, the Catholics in Japan who had managed to defy the edict and maintain their faith had gathered within the castle in Osaka under the protection of the Shogun's main rival. The castle was thought to be impregnable. A tremendous battle ensued that brought Date Masamune back onto the field at the Shogun's side. When it was over, 100,000 bodies littered the fields, and the castle collapsed in flames.

The Shogun prevailed. His power was now absolute and would stay that way for generations. He and Date Masamune, their armor splattered with blood, celebrated the victory together, and the edict against the Catholics was made definitive and irrevocable.

– XXXVI –

In which the Samurais reach St. Tropez, Rosario relies upon her mother,
Guada has a nightmare, and the King is displeased

The Mediterranean thickened further until it resembled a pew-
tery porridge and the clouds lowered and darkened and the
skies began to rumble. During the night, the swells and the wind
increased so that by the time day broke, a fierce storm was upon
them. Men who needed to be on deck were tied to the masts. Many
of those confined below were miserable with fright and sickness.
Unforeseen currents flowing north from Africa pushed the ship off
course toward France.

As the intensity of the storm abated, the ship found calmer waters
the following evening and dropped three anchors off the shore of
Saint-Tropez. Heavy rains fell through the night. But with morning all was clean and fresh, and the warm sun returned, turning the
water blue and transparent again. The Delegation came ashore for
provisions and remained there for three days, causing much sensation among the local populace.

> *They never touch food with their fingers, but instead use two small*
> *sticks that they hold with three fingers. . . . They blow their noses in*
> *soft silky papers the size of a hand, which they never use twice, so that*
> *they throw them on the ground after usage, and they were delighted to*

see our people around them precipitate themselves to pick them up. . . .
Their swords cut so well that they can cut a soft paper just by putting
it on the edge and blowing on it. (*Relations of Mme de St. Tropez*—
October 1615, Bibliothèque Inguimbertine, Carpentras)

But Shiro stayed aboard the ship and passed the time swimming, getting stronger, and attempting to close his fingers around the hilt of his new sword.

***

With Shiro gone, Rosario asked her mother to move in with her at the finca. Her father had died the year before of a broken back, slipping in the mountains while pursuing a goat. Her two brothers were in Cádiz seeking their fortunes, and her two sisters had married men from Arcos de la Frontera. Her ex-husband, Antonio, had remarried, to a girl from the village Rosario had never liked and who had yet to become pregnant.

Her mother, Carmen, had not been in the Duke's residence for twenty years. It had been her own pregnancy—when carrying Rosario—that had persuaded the Duke to end it with her. This happened at a time when he spent long periods away from his ancestral home.

'It was when he returned from the disastrous Armada that he first took a liking to me and it lasted for seven years. I remember the house as being much larger, but I suppose that is normal.'

They were walking through the mansion, from wing to wing, from salon to salon, through the well-raked gardens and into the chapel.

They paused in the kitchen where some who worked there knew mother and daughter from the village.

They took their evening meal by a small fire in the dining hall at the table where the Duke had lashed out at Doña Inmaculada and Guada. Then they retired to the master bedroom, where they lay down next to each other on the high massive bed. Both of them, decades apart, had experienced hours of intimacy with him there. Neither of them referred to it, but both had it in mind. They lay in silence, taking it all in until Rosario began to laugh. Carmen smiled and said, '*Vaya por Dios*,' and began to laugh, as well.

After Rosario fell asleep, Carmen rose and walked to the window. The village below was dark with only the church tower visible in the moonlight. In the hills above she heard a lynx howling in heat. She felt a chill. She was the only soul who knew for sure that Rosario was the Duke's daughter, and she closed her eyes for a long moment to pray to Mary, asking that God not punish her silence by cursing them with a damaged child.

***

One hundred and twenty-five kilometers away, in Sevilla, Guada was awake, as well. Her abdomen had grown to the point where she needed to get up more often throughout the night. Her room at Soledad's palacete was lavish. Her aunt had chosen it on purpose, hoping it would help keep her niece there and serve to underline Guada's sense of belonging to an impeccable bloodline.

Shiro's last letter had moved her deeply and made her all too aware of her true feelings for him. And though she was glad for him, glad to learn he had rejoined his compatriots and thus the world, glad to think he had left the lugubrious finca in Medina-Sidonia and its comely mistress, she felt an ache in her heart. For the distance between them now was vast again. The farthest that she had ever journeyed had been to Madrid, many years ago. The recent travels to Medina-Sidonia and to Sanlúcar de Barrameda had been dramatic events in her young life. Most people she knew, including Julian, including her mother and her aunt, had hardly traveled, either. But Shiro had come from the other side of the Earth and was now on his way to Italy to meet with the Holy Father. Afterwards he would return to Madrid once more before leaving for Japan.

In the letter he had written, 'Though I rebel against the notion, I realize there is a good chance we shall never see each other again. Where, Guada, is your sense of fate when I most require it? Or is this what your fates had in store? For us to meet, to dream of a possibility, in my case at least, and then to part forever?'

She considered his question valid and only wished that it be his definition of fate that would somehow prevail, the one in which one's will predominated. That they could have some sort of a future together was, of course, impossible, unthinkable. But she did wish to see him again, if only to prove to herself he was not an invention of her battered spirit.

She was reluctant to go back to sleep. It comforted her to know her aunt was just down the hall, the servants in their quarters, that she was safe. She had awakened from an unpleasant dream in which Julian had again been forcing himself upon her. She could not make out his features but felt his weight and urgency and though she fought to get him off her, her limbs were heavy and barely responsive, the way Shiro had described his damaged fingers to be. She had only been able to raise her head enough to see her mother seated in a chair beside the bed, filled with mirth and urging the beast on. Guada had begun to scream until Julian finally looked at her, as if to tell her to be quiet. But as he did, she saw that his face was different, it was the face of her father Rodrigo and she had awakened from the dream whimpering and in a sweat. Reaching for the chamber pot she began to pray immediately, cursing the Devil for having toyed with her so cruelly. And she remembered how in the dream the pillow where her head had thrashed back and forth was embroidered with the letters M and V entwined together, stitched in blue thread. All she could think of was the Virgin Mother, or was it Marta Vélez?

She was in no hurry to return to sleep. She was content to sit by her window enjoying the night jasmine and to wait for the first light of day.

***

Philip the Third decreed a week of hunting for young noblemen on the grounds of the Pardo Palace. It was the Duke of Lerma's idea that he and the King make a concentrated effort to get to know the up-and-coming young men who would soon be replacing fathers too old or infirm to continue journeying and contributing to the Royal coffers.

Two days into the event, the King was already bored and impatient, and he complained to the Duke of Lerma for having made the affair three days too long. The Duke in turn blamed it on an underling and promised the Monarch it would never occur again. At the end of the third, raucous meal, set out on long tables in the countryside, the King left early, unconvincingly begging their collective pardon, claiming to be overly burdened by pressing matters of state. All rose and bowed and toasted his good health.

The Duke of Lerma stood by as the King mounted his steed. Surrounded by a dozen mounted soldiers and followed by pages, priests, and secretaries, the ruler of the world's largest empire set out, relieved to return to the palace. But just as they were about to break free of the area, something caught his eye. He reined in his horse and raised his hand for all to do likewise. The Duke trotted up beside him. 'Sire?'

At the outer perimeter of the clearing chosen for the meal, all of the horses belonging to the young nobles were gathered. They were tied to posts and branches and next to each horse saddles and hunting gear rested on the grass guarded by faithful servants, some of whom had accompanied their masters from distant parts of the kingdom. Strapped to one of the saddles was a red leather quiver filled with arrows.

'There,' pointed the King. 'The red quiver—fetch it to me.'

Instructions were shouted, and within seconds a soldier stood beside the Royal stallion holding the quiver in both hands for the Monarch's inspection. The King leaned down and took a good look at it. There could be no two like it in the world and certainly not in Spain. And the arrows bore the markings of his own master archer, a skilled *Jinense* inherited from his father Philip II.

The King turned to the Duke of Lerma. 'Find the man that saddle belongs to, and bring him to me immediately.'

– PART FOUR –

- PART FOUR -

– XXXVII –

In which the Pope is sly

Camillo Borghese received them in the Map Room. He was seated on an elevated throne flanked by Cardinals and sixty members of the Swiss Guard in full array. The setting, with its enormous, vivid frescoes painted by Ignazio Danti, was calibrated to present an image of spiritual magnificence and geographical domination. Father Sotelo, in a state of high excitement, beamed at the surroundings as if to say to his Asian guests, '*This* is where I come from. *This* is what I and my God represent.'

Excerpt from an account written by Father Luis Sotelo, *De ecclesiae Iaponicae statu relatio*:

> *When we got there by the aid of God in the Year of Our Salvation 1615, not only were we kindly received by His Holiness the great Pope, with the Holy College of the Cardinals and a gathering of bishops and nobles, and even the joy and general happiness of the Roman People, but we and three others (whom the Japanese Christians had specially designated to announce their condition with respect to the Christian religion) were heard, rested, and just as we were hoping, dispatched as quickly as possible.*

Hasekura Tsunenaga and Shiro, impressed as they were, privately judged the enormous hall to be ostentatious and overdone. They preferred the luxurious austerity displayed in Philip the Third's Spain. The baroque papal presentation did not intimidate them, for they had the throne rooms in Edo and in Kyoto and in Osaka for use as comparison, rooms that derived their splendor from exquisite design and a minimal intrusion of furniture. Nevertheless, they bowed repeatedly and rendered a convincing show of awe and modesty in the hope it would help obtain the realization of Date Masamune's wishes.

Translation of the Latin letter from Date Masamune to the Pope:

> *Kissing the Holy feet of the Great, Universal, Most Holy Lord of The Entire World, Pope Paul, in profound submission and reverence, I, Date Masamune, King of Sendai in the Empire of Japan, suppliantly say: The Franciscan Padre Luis Sotelo came to our country to spread the faith of God. On that occasion, I learnt about this faith and desired to become a Christian, but I still haven't accomplished this desire due to some small issues. However, in order to encourage my subjects to become Christians, I wish that you send missionaries of the Franciscan church. I guarantee that you will be able to build a church and that your missionaries will be protected. I also wish that you select and send a bishop as well. Because of that, I have sent one of my samurai, Hasekura Tsunenaga, as my representative to accompany Luis Sotelo across the seas to Rome, to give you a stamp of obedience and to kiss your feet. Further, as our country and Nueva España are neighbouring countries, I beg your intervention so that we can discuss with the King of Spain, for the benefit of dispatching missionaries across the seas.*

The Pope seemed receptive and genuinely curious, and he agreed to the dispatch of additional missionaries to Japan and sanctioned the idea of Sotelo's church. But on the topic of trade, he decided to defer to Philip the Third.

'When you return to Madrid, tell the King you have my blessing and that I shall defer to his decisions in all matters nonspiritual.'

It was a start, or so they convinced themselves. Hasekura Tsunenaga's portrait was painted by Claude Deruet, and the Ambassador was made an honorary citizen of Rome. Shiro was pained and surprised to hear Date Masamune's recognition of Father Sotelo's desire for a church to be built in Sendai and hoped it was a ruse. The language employed in the letter to the Pope was most unlike him, and Shiro clung to that.

At the reception afterwards, Cardinal Roberto Bellarmino, prompted by Father Sotelo, paused to speak with Shiro, who told him that the King of Spain had made him a gift of the Cardinal's book, the 'Doctrina Cristiana.' Flattered to the core and after an extended exchange of pleasantries, the Cardinal took an interest in the young man's damaged hands.

'I have an acquaintance who may be of use to you, an astronomer with an artistic bent who has many friends among the best doctors and surgeons in Rome. I shall have you presented to him if you so desire, but on one condition.'

'My Lord?' Shiro asked.

'That you not allow him to addle your soul with his sinful rant about the Earth not being at the center of the universe.'

– XXXVIII –

In which two dogs eat chestnuts

A messenger from the Duke of Lerma arrived at Don Rodrigo's house in Sevilla summoning the Grandee to Madrid for a meeting with the King. Rodrigo could barely contain his excitement at the thought he was about to be awarded some special mission. Doña Inmaculada intuited another possibility.

'The audience might have something to do with Guada,' she said.

'Guada?' he asked incredulously. 'He's barely aware of her existence.'

'She spent three years at court and was well received.'

'But what would that possibly have to do with this? You don't send a rider on a four-day journey to Sevilla to bring back a Grandee of Spain to conference with his King about our daughter.'

'Perhaps you're right,' she said affecting a pallid smile. She saw no point in going on about it.

'Of course I'm right,' he said.

'We'll know soon enough,' she replied.

He entered the capital at twilight at the end of a clear November's day and went directly to Marta Vélez's mansion, where he was greeted sympathetically. Not wishing to contemplate any connection she might have with the royal summons, she instead encouraged Rodrigo in his fantasies about what might be on the King's mind. An ambassadorship would be the most likely explanation, and to somewhere important, France perhaps, or the Low Countries.

On his way to the Alcázar the following morning, he was already making mental calculations regarding the allocation of household funds and the choosing of favored employees who might keep a proper eye on his estates during his time abroad. The Duke of Lerma greeted him warmly but when questioned pleaded ignorance, a response that only served to intensify Rodrigo's curiosity given the universally acknowledged belief that the Duke of Lerma knew everything about the Monarch.

Rodrigo was ushered into the Royal Library. It contained hundreds of volumes assembled for the King by a committee of *sabios* or wise men, who had been charged with the task of putting together a selection of titles aimed at helping the Monarch pilot the ship of state. But Philip had also insisted the library contain works banned by the Holy Office of the Inquisition, one of which, *The Memoirs of Benvenuto Cellini*, he was enjoying when Rodrigo appeared. Two large dogs rose from the floor and approached the Grandee as he bowed to the King.

'Your Majesty.'

'Don Rodrigo. I am so pleased you could come. Don't mind the dogs. They prefer chestnuts to flesh, and I've a bowlful here,' he said, pointing to a valuable ceramic resting by the opened manuscript.

'Chestnuts, sire . . .'

'They are *Canes de Palleiro*, from Galicia—chestnut trees all over the place.'

'A province unknown to me, I'm afraid,' said Rodrigo with a grin.

'You old snob,' replied the King. 'I doubt you're afraid to say it at all. To men like yourself it must seem like a black forest filled with Visigoths, not an olive grove or a jasmine vine within hundreds of kilometers.'

'It does have a reputation, sire.'

The King tossed a pair of polished chestnuts into the air, and the dogs caught them in midflight. Rodrigo appreciated the touch of how the animals, gruff beasts that would have been more in place in a corral in the rainy north, nevertheless wore silken collars embroidered with the Hapsburg coat of arms.

'The sun does shine there occasionally,' said the King, 'and if you don't mind a bit of damp, the hunting to be had is far superior to anything around here.'

'As you know, sire, hunting has never been my strong point. I prefer the relative comforts of husbandry.'

'I know. I know,' said the King, irritated, and Rodrigo picked up on it. 'Your degree of *civilization* is most impressive.'

'Not at all, sire. I only meant . . .'

'In any event,' said the King, interrupting Rodrigo's worried apology, 'it's the topic of "husbandry" in fact that has led me to ask you back to Madrid, and for that it is I who must apologize. But I find myself in a potentially delicate situation.'

'The journey is inconsequential, My Lord,' said Rodrigo, hoping to get things back on a better track. 'I am here to serve.'

There was something in the Monarch's tone and body language that caused Rodrigo to realize that an ambassadorship would probably not be on the day's agenda.

'How do you feel about your son-in-law Julian? What opinion of him have you? And take a seat, man.'

The dogs had resettled themselves next to the King's chair. One looked as if it might already be asleep while the other vigorously scratched at its neck with a hind paw. Rodrigo sat opposite the King, on a chair slightly lower than the Monarch's. On the table between them were Cellini's opened codex and the Moorish bowl of shiny nuts. For the life of him and as an indication of his general obtuseness, Rodrigo could not fathom why the King might have taken an interest in Julian, and he strained to respond with what would be the correct answer.

'I must confess, sire, and at the cost of some embarrassment, that I do not know the boy all that well. My wife has often accused me of being a distant parent.'

'The "boy" as you call him, is now very much a man as far as I am concerned. Surely you must have some inkling of an impression as to his nobility, and by that I am not referring to his lineage.'

'Understood, my lord. Well, I would say, I might say, that it seems that sometimes he may exhibit somewhat temperamental qualities.'

'Temperamental.'

'Pique, anger, mixed with a certain hubristic bravado.'

Though the foul event claimed and protested by his daughter did cross his mind at this point, what he was most remembering with a much heftier dose of spite was the sound of the laughter he had heard from the boy and Marta Vélez on that night, now over a year ago, as he had clambered back down the tree in front of her bedroom window.

213

'I've had him arrested,' said the King.

'Arrested?'

'He's here in the dungeon of the palace, in an area well aired and attended that is reserved for the nobility, but in chains.'

'*Virgen Santo!*' said the Grandee. 'Why, sire?'

'I will get to that in a minute. I've called you here for two reasons. First of all, his own father is old and ill. As you probably know, after a clutch of daughters Julian came along late in his parents' life. I've never met the father, although my father and I have always been grateful for the taxes collected from their vast estates, some of which now belong to you. But he is not a Grandee. You, my friend, are in a different sphere altogether, and so I feel I have an obligation to warn you of the embarrassment the young fellow's crimes might bring upon you and your family unless you disown him quickly.'

'I see.'

'Second of all, I was hoping you might corroborate a tale I've learned thanks to a most shocking letter I asked for and received last week from the recently widowed woman who married our beloved Duke of Medina-Sidonia, a letter that led to my asking you here.'

Inmaculada had been right. As his face reddened, Rodrigo unreasonably cursed the woman while simultaneously marveling at her perspicacity.

'Might this have something to do with my daughter, sire?'

'It does.'

'I see.'

'The letter states she was violated against her will by her own husband. Are you aware of this?'

'Yes.'

'And did you confront him about it?'

'No, sire. It is a delicate matter,' Rodrigo said, looking down.

'Perhaps such a thing is ignored or even encouraged by the heathens of this world,' said the King, 'but it is not sanctioned in this realm by our Holy Mother Church, nor by me, who am the Church's defender.'

'I am aware of that, sire."

'Now, I realize it can be a delicate matter, as you put it. Such acts are inevitably committed in private and rarely have witnesses and come to depend on the sole testimony of the victim. But I must ask. How did you and your wife react when you learned of it?'

'We counseled forbearance, my lord. We saw no advantage in airing such intimacies.'

'An honest answer. I appreciate that.'

'Why sire, might I ask, are you this concerned with this particular case?'

'Two reasons,' said the King. 'I have learned of it firsthand and therefore cannot look away from it. If that were all and you were to plead for me to share in you and your wife's counsel of forbearance, I might have acceded. But I cannot, especially because I have such fond memories of the years Guada spent here at court. She was a favorite of our late Queen. The idea of her being subjected to such a thing is abhorrent to me. But that is my second reason. My first reason, in all honesty, is that I first became aware of this sad tale in a manner most offensive to my person.'

Rodrigo was appalled and enraged at having his own opinions questioned, his role as a father disparaged, nay, insulted and overlooked by the inbred gentleman across from him who had more Teuton blood in his veins than Iberian.

'I am humbled, my lord,' he said.

The King went on.

'The late Duke of Medina-Sidonia was much beloved in this palace. He put up with immense challenges and even ridicule because of my father's occasional pigheadedness, and he did so without ever losing his sense of grace or humor, ever the gentleman, ever the elegant warrior. In the final months of his life, he acquired a most unusual protégé, a young man, a Prince I'm told, from the distant realm of Japan, a young man of unusual distinction and taste I took a liking for, as well, and to whom I had commissioned a special gift that only he would truly appreciate. This young man left court shortly afterwards, of a sudden, and was not heard from again. Then some weeks ago while entertaining a generation of younger noblemen at a hunt organized by the Duke of Lerma I saw the gift, a red leather quiver filled with arrows from my personal supply. It was brought to the hunt by none other than your son-in-law, and when I questioned him about it, as to how he had come to acquire it, he lied to me, repeatedly, lied to my face.'

Rodrigo felt lost, like he was sinking, as if tossed from a ship into the sea.

'The story, according to the letter I received,' said the King, 'goes like this. . .'

Relying on Rosario's detailed account, taken down and neatly transcribed by the same gentleman who had helped Shiro with his first letters to Guada, the King then proceeded to tell the tale, beginning with Shiro's befriending of Diego Molina aboard the Date Maru and ending with the heinous rape of Guada and her subsequent pregnancy. He also described the multifaceted role Marta Vélez had played in the affair.

'I'm afraid your mistress has much to be sorry for,' he said in conclusion.

'I had no idea she was still entertaining Julian,' Rodrigo said, if only to say something, anything at all, while the full weight of the account along with its possible consequences made its way through the conduits of his brain.

'I've called you here to corroborate some facts,' said the King, 'one of which, the aggression against your daughter, you have already confirmed. Is she in fact pregnant?'

'Yes, Your Majesty.'

'And living I understand with Soledad Medina.'

'That is correct.'

'Because you would not accede to her complaint.'

'We saw no point, especially when the pregnancy was discovered.'

'And there was the question of the estates accrued to you because of her marriage.'

'That, too, sire.'

'Once again, I respect your honesty, Rodrigo.'

'Sire.'

A momentary silence gripped the room in a vise.

'May I ask, sire,' Rodrigo finally said, 'what you are going to do with him?'

'The charge of murder against the sailor or the olive worker or whatever he was is the most grievous one,' said the King. 'There were witnesses to it, two thugs who helped him carry it out. Both of them confessed. One of them did not survive his confession, but the other is still with us and was also present on the evening my young friend from Japan was assaulted, and this thug has also testified he heard Guada's screams both during and after that event. I also know from my own guards that the young Samurai, now in Rome, has virtually lost the use of his hands. You ask me what I am going to do with Julian. . .'

Here the King paused and stared into the flames before them.

'You know,' he then said in a quieter tone, 'I could have brooked almost anything from the cad, if only out of respect for you and for his aging father. But his lying to me the way he did, lies I now have had validated from sufficient sources, is unforgiveable.'

'Of course,' Rodrigo said. Then, somewhat wistfully, he added, 'With my own son's embrasure of chastity and the cross I had looked forward in Julian to having another.'

'That was a mistake,' said the King. 'But Perhaps Guada's child will be a son, and you can spend your remaining years taking good care of them. She and the child, whatever its sex, shall inherit all of Julian's holdings. I'll see to that. As to what to do with him,' he concluded, petting the sleeping dog, 'I've decided to leave that up to the Samurai.'

– XXXIX –

In which Shiro takes a Roman bath

Edo and Kyoto were brown and white with green leaves and spindly flowering trees in spring and gray paths of raked pebbles. Madrid was orange and tan with burnt roofs and slate steeples and acacia blossoms late in summer. And Rome, Shiro thought, was salmon and ochre and overripened lemon, veined marble and stones smoothened with time, frescoes deep blue and cloaks the color of blood. It was close to the winter solstice, and the Tiber flowed high and full. The city smelled of drainage and debauchery, intimacy and incense. Citizens huddled by fires lit beside the ruins of its golden age.

Galileo Galilei invited the Samurai to a supper party in a villa owned by the physicist's friend, Federico Cesi, Prince of St. Angelo and St. Polo. The enormous house, surrounded by umbrella pines and equipped with a still functioning 2nd century bath, dominated the top of the Gianicolo. From a wide veranda dotted with statues of naked goddesses, one could see many of the city's most prominent buildings. The gathering commenced while there was still sufficient light to peer through Galileo's telescope, by which one could clearly discern the letters chiseled into the distant facade of San Giovanni in Laterno. After supper a number of the guests attempted to find the moons of Jupiter but owing perhaps to the amount of spirits consumed, only with middling success.

Galileo had never made the acquaintance of anyone from the Far East. Shiro's command of Latin, Greek, English, and Spanish astonished him, and he took delight in showing him off to the others. When the topic of his heretical theory came up as it inevitably did in those years, and with his tongue loosened that night by a liter of Chianti, the visionary held forth. Though he was addressing himself to Shiro, he made a point of directing his gaze to the others, as well.

'Bellarmino is a Neanderthal who in that age might well have protested the invention of the wheel.'

Shiro maintained an impassive smile as the others laughed aloud.

'I've little doubt he would have found a way to declare it sacrilegious. All I've tried to do is stand upon the shoulders of Nicolaus Copernicus, who stood upon the shoulders of Philolaus, Heraclides Ponticus, Aristarchus of Samos, the Islamic astronomer Nasir al-Din al-Tusi, and the Indian mathematician Aryabhata.'

This was accompanied by cheers, even from those, the majority, with no idea who the historical figures being mentioned were.

'Astronomy has played a key role in my culture and in its two central religions,' Shiro said, 'in Shintoism and Buddhism. Wise men from China have had a long influence on our astronomical observations, on our astrological calendar. But unlike you, I have no great names to cite. It has simply been a part of who we are, for as long as anyone can remember. But no one, as far as I know, has suffered because of any competing beliefs about the machinations of the stars.'

At first Galileo was irked at the interruption, but when his persecution by the Church was alluded to, all was forgiven.

'As you can see by my surroundings here this evening, young man, I am not suffering too much, either,' Galileo said, aiming his cup of wine at his friends to more laughter. 'Yes, I am ahead of my time, but I've learned my place. It's certainly not worth being tortured for. What the Church refuses to acknowledge will be a common fact after my death, and they will be embarrassed by it. So though I am shunned and isolated now, I have, as you can see, many good friends, and there are advantages to being on the outside of things.'

'Hear! Hear!' someone cried.

Shiro thought it rude and unbecoming that the physicist had paid no mind to the Samurai's words concerning the status of astronomy in Japan.

'I'll wager that when you return to the East, young man, you will feel the same way,' Galileo went on. 'This journey you have made and your knowledge of language is going to change you in ways that will only become apparent when you return. It happened to me by simply moving from Pisa to Rome!'

More laughter followed along with a prolonged fit of coughing from a short fat man who nevertheless did not cease chewing on a leg of chicken.

'Now let us have a look at those hands,' concluded the physicist. And at that a number of men and a few of the women gathered around the Samurai.

Shiro by then had mastered the ability to close his hands about the hilt of his sword, but he was unable to squeeze them tight enough for fighting. He had regained strength in his arms, but most of his fingers were still plagued with a tingling numbness that came and went. One of the doctors present suggested a system of leather straps that might be attached to one another with small buckles and that would force the damaged hands into a more rigid grip.

Late in the evening, there was music and revelry, and one of the women approached Shiro. They spoke for a time and went as far as sharing a bath in the ancient *balnea romani*. Under the hot water and lit by torches, he admired its floor covered with small tiles depicting sea horses. But since bidding farewell to Rosario, he noticed how his interest in other women waned because of his correspondence with Guada.

He gently put the *puella* off and, wrapped in towels, was content to lie back on a pallet gazing at the stars until dawn, listening to the merrymakers on the veranda. He thought them a wise, easygoing, provincial group, content within the familiarity of their singular city, paying scant attention to his own condition, as far that night from home as he would ever be, on the far side of the moon, at the outermost limit, poised on the verge of return.

– XL –

In which Guada returns home

Rodrigo left for Sevilla directly from the Alcázar. He did not return to Marta Vélez's house. He would never return there again. The anger he felt toward the woman who had been his mistress for five years, though aided and abetted by the role she had played in his daughter's misery, was primarily due to his having discovered, from the King no less, that Marta had continued to lie with his son-in-law. She had sworn to him that the dalliance with her nephew had come to an end; that she had grown bored to tears with the lad. The vigor she displayed, at least at the beginning, when renewing her sympathies for the Grandee had been convincing. But clearly her unseemly lust for Julian had continued. He would not allow her the satisfaction of making a fool of him again.

Riding down through the flatlands of La Mancha and Valdepeñas, down through the vertiginous wilds of Despeñaperros and on to Córdoba, he spent profligately, inviting himself into the best homes, bestowing lavish gifts upon his hosts, eating and imbibing in excess. Stopping at Soledad Medina's estate, La Moratalla, where Guada and Julian had passed their honeymoon, he lingered for two full days and nights, making repeated and useless attempts to bed down a servant girl. Considering himself to be once again a single man, for Doña Inmaculada did not figure into it, he felt both the power and the dread of his new status. It dizzied him. And he was no longer the man he had been when he first began courting Marta Vélez. He wished to prove something by getting his way with the servant girl and thus was doubly humiliated when she turned down his charms, the power of his station, and finally an exorbitant offer of silver to give in to him. But she had said no and at one moment called him '*un abuelito*.'

He arrived in Sevilla despondent, put out to pasture, feeling gray and unappealing, his run as a Don Juan at an end. He rode directly to Doña Soledad's palacete, for he was not yet ready to bear the scourge of what would be Inmaculada's volcanic derision, congratulating herself for having been right about why the King had summoned him. He hoped that by doing the right thing by his daughter, taking the bull by the horns, his wife's spite might be diluted.

He found Soledad's residence almost irritatingly superior to his own. It occurred to him that years had passed since his last visit there. The condition of her gardens and carriages, the gravel of the front drive, the magnificent facade, the understatement and luxurious quality of the floor tiles in the entranceway, the paintings, the ferns cleanly and simply planted in plain terracotta pots placed at either side of the stairwells. Was she that much wealthier than he, or worse, simply endowed with better taste and the will to exercise it consistently? He would have to speak with Inmaculada about this once the storm had passed.

He waited in the sitting room, exhausted from the journey, fully aware that he looked unpresentable and in need of a bath. As their footsteps approached, he rose to greet them.

'Rodrigo,' said Doña Soledad. 'What a pleasant surprise.'

He found her looking inexplicably fit, beautifully dressed, her white hair perfectly coiffed. What impressed him more was the evidence of his daughter's advanced state as she curtsied to him, keeping one hand over her swollen abdomen.

The women knew of course that he had been called to Madrid but made no mention of it, nor did they express any misgivings at his semiwild appearance. Salutations were exchanged and refreshments brought. It was only then that Rodrigo came to the point. He took his daughter's hand and, doing so, felt a stab of emotion that cut him to the quick.

'Julian has been arrested by the King's guards in Madrid. The King has stripped him of all his goods and claims and is having them signed over to you. I've come to take you home, or to your own home if you so desire, for it is now yours, free and clear as it always should have been, and for that I deeply apologize.'

After sending a message to Inmaculada asking her to meet them, they took Soledad's finest carriage and proceeded to Guada's house, where she had not set foot since the fateful evening. The servants still in residence who had joined the household as part of Julian's retinue were told to return to Valencia. Those who had come with Guada upon her marriage, some of whom had been with her since her birth, were embraced and asked to pack up any- and everything that belonged to her husband. Guada then instructed that the room where the assault upon her had taken place be disassembled, re-painted, and used from that day forward exclusively for storage. She also ordered that the entrance patio where Shiro had been wounded be retiled, its lemon and orange trees pulled out, and that the seeds he had given her be planted in their place.

Don Rodrigo and Doña Soledad made a list of the changes and then settled down in a corner to a serious conversation in which he related all he had learned in Madrid. Inmaculada sat with Guada and insisted that she rest. They retired to the library. Guada did feel weary, but she was elated, and sad, and suspicious. Although she wished to feel close to her parents again, a distance had installed itself between them that was new and perhaps insurmountable. She realized that the bulk of her familial affection had been transferred to her aunt.

It was only as the last batch of items pertaining to Julian were being carried down the stairs, to be loaded onto a cart waiting in the street, that Guada suddenly came back to life. She rose and asked the men to halt because she saw something sticking from the gathered gear she knew had nothing to do with her husband. Reaching in carefully as her mother and father and aunt looked on, she removed Shiro's Daisho, the Tanto that had been used against him to wound his shoulder and cut off his finger, and the prized Katana given to him by Date Masamune.

226

– LVI –

In which Shiro regains a quiver

Barcelona, honor of Spain, alarm and terror of enemies near and far, luxury and delight of its inhabitants, refuge of foreigners, school of chivalry, and epitome of all that a civilized and inquisitive taste could ask for in a great, famous, rich and well founded city.

—Miguel de Cervantes Saavedra

They returned to Barcelona on calm seas and without incident. As they neared the shore, Father Sotelo held forth for Shiro and Hasekura Tsunenaga about the origin of the city's name. He first reviewed certain basics of Greek and Roman mythology the Japanese gentlemen found far more engaging than the tales contained in the Christian tomes they'd been made to study.

'Hercules joined forces with Jason and his Argonauts,' the Friar then said, 'in search of the Golden Fleece. From Greece they traversed the Mediterranean in nine ships, but one was lost in a storm off the coast of Catalunya, just where we are now. Hercules went in search of it and found the ship wrecked and unsalvageable, but the crew was safe and sound, and all of them were so taken by the beauty of the coast and the interior terrain they named it *Barca Nona*, or the Ninth Ship.'

As their own vessel docked at the harbor, it coincided with a fishing sloop weighing anchor that presented the Delegation with a most novel and vulgar scene. While the fishermen hauled sails and got underway, some of the women waving good-bye on shore pulled up their skirts and opened their legs, purposely exposing their intimacies. A crewmember on the Delegation's deck local to the area provided the explanation. 'There is an old saying that goes back hundreds of years,' he said with a grin. '*La mar es posa bona—si veu el cony d'una dona.*' (The sea calms down—if it sees a woman's c___.)

Not invulnerable to superstition, Shiro made sure to step off the gangway with his left foot first. As he felt the land under him again, his thoughts turned more ardently than ever toward Sevilla and Guada. He was anxious to reach Madrid, from where he might renew their correspondence. Hasekura Tsunenaga came up to him on the pier.

'The next ship we board will be one taking us home.'

Five days later they entered Segovia on horseback in the middle of a snowstorm. But when they awakened the following morning, a warm sun shone, and by noon the snow had disappeared. They reached Madrid early that evening. Shiro was summoned by the King soon afterwards. So as not to insult Hasekura Tsunenaga, the page sent to fetch the young Samurai was under instruction to approach him only if he was alone. It was late at night when they met in the King's private quarters. The two men sat by the hearth, where a crackling fire burned thick logs of dried olive wood. The dogs were absent.

'I have been appraised of your audience with the Holy Father, and I am compelled to tell you I've learned that certain events of importance have transpired in Japan since you left its shores. I now know that your Lord, Date Masamune, though a powerful, brave, and honorable man, a benevolent ruler of vast territory, and head of a large army, is not the recognized ruler of the Japanese kingdom and that the credentials brought to me and the Pope should have originated from Tokugawa Ieyasu and his son. This at least is the formal excuse I shall present to Hasekura Tsunenaga tomorrow to justify my refusal to sign a pact of trade. I say excuse because the real reason is far more grave. Word has reached us of an edict proclaimed and carried out last year by the Shogun that has outlawed Christians and Christianity in Japan. We are not yet clear on the details, but apparently something dramatic occurred that led to it. The Church's missionaries are now in mortal danger. I will be sorry to disappoint Hasekura Tsunenaga and the Lord who sent you here with the best intentions. I wished for you to be the first to know.'

Shiro was flattered by the gesture and was surprised to find himself relieved by the King's pronouncement. Would Date Masamune and the Shogun be disappointed? Perhaps they no longer cared. Who knew what had been going on at home all this time? But he himself felt a long-borne burden ease. The Christian preaching was a nuisance, a confusion, and an affront to the traditions he came from. The crosses and halos, the insistence on complicated biblical mythologies imported from a distant desert, were an awkward, untenable intrusion on his native soil. He wished to think of it as a place where plum blossoms, silence, the sound of running water, the scent of tea, and the pureness of snow were more valued than an eternal life in some imaginary realm above the clouds. But so as not to insult the King, he said none of this and merely replied, 'I can only respect the wisdom of your decision, Your Majesty.'

The King waved this aside. 'I have also learned of your misfortune, Shiro-San, of what happened to you and why.'

The King noted how the Samurai, upon hearing this, instinctively hid his hands within the sleeves of his robe.

'My advisors, the Duke of Lerma, and many in the nobility think it odd I pay your presence such attention. They don't say it to me in so many words, of course, but I can see it. But they lack a King's perspective. They are incapable of seeing how unusual it is that someone who has come from a community of warriors from such a distant culture as yours has your sensitivity to our Western art, our Christian values, and our way of life. I see in you a sort of young man I aspired to become when I was your age but that I was unable to achieve. I expect Alonso saw it, too. I knew him well, you see, and revered him from my childhood. He epitomized a Spanish ideal one so rarely encounters anymore, that teeters, I fear, on the verge of extinction. So I feel obliged to take care of those who were close to him.'

'I am most honored,' Shiro said, somewhat confused.

'I've something for you,' said the King, standing up. Shiro rose from his chair, as well. The King reached behind a large basket filled with kindling and retrieved the red leather quiver and its arrows. He handed it to Shiro.

'I thought you might like to have this back,' said the King.

A mixture of wonder and hatred shot through the Samurai's heart.

'Your Majesty . . .'

'He was foolish enough to bring it with him on a Royal Hunt. When I noticed it and queried him, he lied to me about its provenance. It led to the unraveling of a most dire tale—and to his immediate arrest for the murder of your friend, for what he had his thugs do to you, and for what he did to Doña Guada whom my late wife the Queen was so very fond of.'

'Arrested, you say.'
    'Chained to a wall in the bowels of this very building.'

– XLII –

In which three women have private thoughts

In Coria del Río, Piedad did the best she could to hide her disappointment after the foreigner's disappearance. Finding his battered body washed up on the muddy bank of the Guadalquivir, nursing him back to health, and all that had transpired between them had introduced a miraculous dimension into her life she feared to be already over.

Two months afterwards, she married a man who was her cousin. Her husband was kind except for when he drank, and she expected that soon she would be with child and take her place within the traditional *arras* of the village. But in private moments, she would often remember her discovery of the wounded warrior, her water-logged Odysseus on the coast of Phaeacia. As he had never promised her anything, she could not rebuke him for having left her. But still she fantasized how their life might have been together.

For a while, at the beginning, when his hands and the knife wound were slowly mending, it had all been simple. There had been the changing light of the day, the taste of food, the excitement and comfort of touch. What was it about life, she wondered, that caused it to complicate and tire so quickly? Why were the elementary things, so gloriously sufficient at the start, never enough in the end?

***

Rosario sang her son to sleep, never tiring of observing resemblances between him and the late Duke. She called him her *tesoro*, '*mi tesorito*' in public, and when alone with him her '*picha de oro.*' She missed the Duke and missed the time she had spent with Shiro and wondered what would become of her. Don Alonso's oldest son, Juan Manuel, was now the 8th Duke of Medina-Sidonia, and his son would one day be the 9th. Nevertheless, barring war or a return of the plague, both she and her son could look forward to a long and comfortable life with what the Duke had bequeathed to them.

She had only known three men, two more than most of the girls she had grown up with, and all of them had been dramatically different. Antonio had confirmed what the older village women had warned her about, that men were clumsy and sex an unpleasant obligation to be suffered as infrequently as one could manage. Then the Duke appeared, so much older but a gentleman of the highest order, a generous and grateful bedmate who had given her freedom, given her a son and a future. And finally, the foreigner who fulfilled her beyond all expectation. What was left? Where might another man come from, for she knew everyone in the household and everyone in the village. Unless she moved away, there would be no one else. There was always Sevilla, or a small house near the Royal Court in Madrid where her son's life might prosper in unexpected ways, and yet she could not bear the thought of leaving.

***

Guada took to watering the Biwa shoots. When she tried to imagine what Shiro's mother was like, she saw a version of Doña Inmaculada with slanted eyes, dressed in a beautiful robe like the one Hasekura Tsunenaga wore when he first rode into Sevilla. Shiro's mother, she thought, who had conceived and carried him around within her, suckled and tended to him for years only to have him travel to the other side of the world.

On bad days she felt the child within her to be an invasive monster, the curse of Cain. On good days like these she found herself filled with tenderness for it, tenderness that coursed through her like an underground spring.

Julian was lost. He had done terrible things and would pay with his life. What had become of the handsome boy she had played with? It was as if he had been stricken by an illness. Once again she forced herself to revisit the awful fact that she had chosen to marry him and that she had brought these woes upon herself, woes that would be with her and her child for the rest of their lives.

– XLIII –

In which crimes are avenged

Hasekura Tsunenaga took the news of the Shogun's edict hard. At first he chose not to believe it. But after only a minute's reflection, instinct told him it was true. It meant the journey had been for nothing. All of his barbarian religious instruction that had culminated in the grand but humiliating baptism ceremony had been for nothing. His pleading at the feet of the Pope, the endless hours of gibberish shared with Luis Sotelo had been an orgy of wasted time. The months and years away from what was left of his family, the thousands of kilometers of open sea, eating foul food, facing daily perils, the almost indescribable tedium of being made to listen to so many people speaking to him in a foreign tongue—all of it a farce.

When his audience with Philip the Third concluded, and weary from travel, he shunned Father Sotelo and sought commiseration with Shiro.

'I understand how you must feel,' Shiro said to him. 'But I refuse to believe the journey has been in vain. For as long as history shall be written, the name of Hasekura Tsunenaga will be recorded as the first Japanese ambassador to visit Spain and Italy, even France. Despite what you may see as failure, your impressions and tales of all that we

235

have lived and seen since leaving Sendai will be demanded by Tokugawa Ieyasu, the Emperor, by all of the most important men in our
kingdom. Regardless of the edict, Date Masamune shall be in your
debt.'

'You are kind to say so, Shiro-San. And if it be true, perhaps the
stain of my father's crime shall be forgotten.'

'Your father is at peace,' Shiro said. 'Time shall cover his indiscre-
tions with benevolence, and his memory will reflect the fame of his
son. I am sure of it.'

Shiro said these things because he believed them and felt for the
man who had once been his enemy. But he also required a favor.

As punishment for the murder Diego Molina, for the maiming he
had been subjected to, and for the violation of Guada, the King
told Shiro he might choose the manner by which Julian would
be executed: decapitation, the garrote, burning at the stake, or
disembowelment followed by being drawn and quartered. For a
brief moment, Shiro entertained the idea of asking for Julian's
crucifixion, which was how many Christians were executed in Japan. But he thought better of it. Besides, he knew from the moment Julian's existence in the dungeon was announced to him
what he must do.

'I came to his home that evening to fight him to the death. That is
still what I wish.'
    'But what about your condition, your hands?'
    'I've no choice,' Shiro said. 'Honor demands it.'
    'So be it,' said the King.

Apart from a compliment of Royal Guards and a priest, the only other Christians to attend the duel were the Duke of Lerma and the King himself. The Monarch and his chief counselor agreed that if the Samurai prevailed, the spectacle of a foreigner killing a young nobleman might be too much for the public or other members of the nobility to witness, no matter how guilty Julian was. The favor Shiro asked of Hasekura Tsunenaga was that he too be present, to claim Shiro's body should he lose.

The group left the Alcázar before dawn on a cold day at the end of January. They rode west, crossing the Manzanares River and continued for another hour until they came to a clearing in the wilderness. Julian was helped down from his horse and untied. A blessing was conferred upon all present, and food and drink were dispensed as the sun rose.

The nerves and the hour and the business at hand kept conversation to a minimum. When the moment arrived, Shiro asked Hasekura Tsunenaga to pull and fasten the buckles attached to the leather straps he'd brought with him from Rome so that he might take a firm hold of the hilt of his sword.

'It pains me to admit it, Your Majesty,' said Julian, all of a sudden, 'but we all know by now that the foreigner's blade is superior to ours. If this is his idea, or anyone else's, of a fair fight, you might as well hand him a musket to shoot me with and be done with it.'

Shiro translated the statement to Hasekura Tsunenaga.

'Who are you, young man,' replied the Duke of Lerma, 'to speak of a fair fight? You who ran a man through after you had him bound to a tree, you who had this man here grabbed by henchmen and held down for torture and maiming?'

'I was and I remain a Christian, My Lord, loyal to the Church and to my King,' Julian answered. 'A Christian who has always endeavored to defend our faith and our way of life from intrusions by heathens like this one, by any means available.'

He finished the last part of his reply looking at the guards and at the priest, hoping to inspire their sympathy. They averted their gaze and looked toward the ground. But Shiro saw what Julian was up to and wished to remove all obstacles to his revenge.

'I shall trade you then,' the Samurai said. 'My sword for yours.'

A murmur went round the circle of men. Julian had not expected this. The nobility of the gesture irritated him, but not wishing to be sliced in two, he accepted.

It proved impossible to strap both of Shiro's hands about the much shorter hilt of the Christian sword. It was a modified, double-bladed *espada ropera*, a weapon he had no experience with. It weighed twice as much as a Katana and to Shiro's eye looked dull and uncouthly smithed. He was only able to use one hand, and the sword's finger ring was useless to him. The King was perturbed. He feared the worst might happen. But he remained silent, having sworn to himself that he would not speak a word that day until the duel was over.

It started badly for the Samurai. Julian pursued him with frenzied energy, swinging the Katana back and forth. At one point it seemed Shiro was running for his life. But as he ran, he lifted the awkward

Christian weapon in different directions, getting the feel of it. Just as Julian, waxing triumphant, began to laugh at his rival's retreat, Shiro stopped short and turned, and it caught Julian by surprise.

He lifted his arms and began a slicing motion aimed at Shiro's neck. The Samurai deflected it, using the thickest part of the Christian sword close to the hilt. For half a minute, Julian attacked as Shiro stood his ground protecting himself, parrying the Katana's swift motions, one after the other, looking to wear his aggressor out. From where the other men watched, it appeared as if it would only be a matter of time before the foreigner would err and provide an entry for the ceaselessly moving blade. But Shiro held on. The more frantic Julian's attack became, the more his frustration grew. It was the frustration Shiro was counting on. He did not retreat. He remained erect and poised, well planted on his feet, meeting each deadly swipe with practiced precision.

Then, when the opportunity he'd been waiting for arrived, as Julian drew the Katana back in order to initiate yet another blow, Shiro, in a short but powerful motion, using all the strength in his arm, brought the Christian blade down and across, hitting Julian mid-calf, cutting into flesh and breaking the shin bone.

Julian cried out and fell to the ground, shocked by the unexpectedness of it, enraged by the pain. Suddenly drained of strength, his heart filled with terror as he watched his blood seep into the earth.

'I beg of you,' he cried out. 'I do not deserve to die like this.'

There he was surrounded by men, one of them his own King, who were there to see him murdered. The bitterness and cruelty of it were overwhelming. He wished to be back in Marta Vélez's bed falling asleep, back in Guada's arms when the marriage seemed possible. He wanted warm morning air wafting through a window smelling of *azahar* orange blossoms. Instead, he was freezing and encircled like a dog, his leg smashed to bits.

'I beg of you sir,' he called out again.

The men were uncomfortable and embarrassed for him, but his cries grabbed their hearts like talons. Shiro looked down at him, at Diego Molina's murderer, the man who had ruined his hands and stabbed him with his own Tanto, the man who had called him a mongrel, cut off his finger, and had his way with Guada. He looked to the King for guidance, like a gladiator directing his gaze at Caesar.

When Julian saw the Samurai look away, he came up onto his good knee and swept out at him one final time with the Katana, using all of his remaining strength. Shiro sensed it and pivoted away, pivoted around in a circle as he was trained to do, but the Katana's blade was long, and the tip of it caught his shoulder, removing a lump of flesh. As he made a full turn, he stepped on the Christian's hands that were still outstretched, as if they were venomous serpents. Then he leaned down to find an angle and thrust the dull metal Spanish sword into Julian's chest. When he saw the blade emerge from Julian's back he yanked it upwards with all his might, shattering ribs and severing arteries. Then he pulled it free. He released his foot as Julian fell dead upon the ground.

– XLIV –

In which the master remembers and Shiro says good-bye

During the two weeks that followed, Julian was buried, Shiro's wound was treated, and Guada gave birth to a son.

Miguel de Cervantes Saavedra, whose modest house was not far from the Alcázar in Madrid, lay at death's door, drifting in and out of sleep. He was refusing food except for the simplest of *caldos*. Like his most renowned creation, he wandered between delusional and rational worlds. While in the former, he was often convinced the bed he lay upon was on board a ship off the coast of North Africa. He could feel the Mediterranean swells beneath, sense the clear heat of the day, smell the brine, hear sails flapping in want of wind, and he would worry, unsure whether the vessel was making its way toward the shore where he would be jailed anew and forgotten in captivity, or he had already been rescued and, pulling away, was on his way back to Spain. In the latter state when reason still had currency and that tended to occur during the morning hours, what he most enjoyed and took solace from were the sounds of two mourning doves coming through his window, the timbre and rhythm of their plaintive cooing. It ferried him back to childhood summer dawns in Alcalá de Henares, to Rome at first light after a night of love, to autumn afternoons in Napoli gazing out toward Capri.

During those same two weeks, the King and his Duke of Lerma returned to the prosecution of their heretics, recalcitrant Moriscos and Jews, and to bolstering the fragile peace along the northern frontiers of the empire. The Delegation from Japan was forgotten until the night before it was to set forth on its journey back south.

Shiro was summoned once again to the King's private study. Once again they sat by the towering hearth. The dogs were there this time. The Samurai still wore his left arm in a sling.

'How is the shoulder?' the Monarch asked.

'Much improved,' Shiro replied. 'It has ceased to bleed, and there has been no further infection.'

'I am glad to hear of it,' the King said, petting one of the dogs. 'And so you are off tomorrow.'

'Yes, Your Majesty.'

'You are going to miss my son's wedding,' said the King.

'I am sorry for it,' Shiro replied.

'The boy is only ten, his bride thirteen, so I expect they shall have to wait a spell before procreating.'

'Do they get on well?' Shiro asked.

'I'm not even sure they have met each other yet,' said the King, laughing, putting his hands together and raising them toward the vaulted ceiling as if asking God for guidance. Then he reached out and took one of Shiro's hands.

'Chances are we shall never see each other again.'

'Probably not, Sire.'

'One rarely knows with certainty, I suppose, when one is seeing someone for the last time.' He handed Shiro a parchment, folded into an envelope and sealed. 'I want you to keep this with you, in case, for whatever reason, you should change your mind and choose to remain in Spain or anywhere within the empire for that matter. It states that you are under my protection and must be afforded the most generous and respectful treatment.'

Shiro took the envelope and slipped it inside his robe next to the remaining Biwa seeds.

'I am humbled, Your Majesty. It seems a more fitting gift for Hasekura Tsunenaga.'

'I suspect your ambassador never wished to leave his homeland, and since I first set eyes upon him, it was clear to me he had only one serious concern, which was to return to Japan. Your story is a different one.'

Shiro smiled, impressed once again by the Monarch's perspicacity.

'And he shall have his gift, too, of course,' the King added.

'In Japan my people have cast yours out,' Shiro said, looking into the fire, as the dog closest to him rested its snout upon his thigh. 'I am told you have cast out foreigners of different faiths, as well, ones who have lived here for centuries. And yet here we are, sitting together, at ease and on the verge of missing each other's company—if I may speak for myself—two people so different in so many ways.'

'Let us leave all that aside,' answered the King, 'and raise a cup to our late friend the Duke of Medina-Sidonia, and to ask that God grant you a safe journey.'

– XLV –

In which their life begins

When he reached Sevilla, Shiro spent three days searching for Diego Molina's widow, and when he found her he presented himself and told Rocío Sánchez that justice had been done. It was only then that he allowed himself to make his way to Soledad Medina's palacete. There he was informed that Doña Guada had moved back into her own residence. By the time he arrived there, it was late in the afternoon, almost twilight. Before knocking on the massive door, he stared at the pavement out front where he had been thrown half-dead almost a year earlier.

Admitted within, he saw at once the beginnings of the Biwa trees surrounded by new tiles. A chambermaid accompanied him upstairs to the room where Guada was feeding her newborn. When she saw him standing there, she blushed and quickly covered her breast with a piece of linen, and in doing so covered the head of the child. At first they said nothing. The chambermaid retreated. All that could be heard was a fountain down in the garden and the baby gorging on his mother's milk.

'You've come,' she finally said.

'Here I am,' he answered.

'Is Julian alive?'

'No,' he said.

She looked away, nodding her head.

'I do not wish to know anything more about it,' she said.

He remained silent until she looked back at him.

'For how long can you stay, here in Sevilla?' she asked.

'Until we know a ship has been readied in Sanlúcar,' he said. 'A matter of weeks.'

Tears came into her eyes. She did not fight them. Without knowing why, she felt as if her life might be leaving her.

'Will you stay here?' she said. 'With me?'

– XLVI –

In which Shiro makes a decision

When they touched each other, when they held hands, when they fell asleep naked in her bed, culture disappeared. When clothed and facing the world, her worried aunt, scandalized servants, her horrified parents, the world returned to them.

She told him how she'd wished her arm had reached under his tent that night in Baelo Claudia. She described the intimate effect he had caused when his knees pressed against hers in the carriage from Medina-Sidonia to Sevilla. At night with the household asleep, they would take the baby and lie out on the upper balcony, staring at the heavens. He told her all he could remember about Japan. They compared memories of childhood summers, his within the gardens of the castle in Sendai, hers amongst the rolling plains surrounding Carmona.

He believed she was made for him, her scent, her skin, the feel of her, the back of her neck, the way she looked at him. Nothing they said or did shamed them. Every posture and every word was a source of pleasure.

And when the time arrived, he went to speak with Hasekura Tsunenaga. He returned the sword the older Samurai had lent to him, and they both admired anew Shiro's recovered blade that had once been a point of contention between them. They walked conversing along the bank of the Guadalquivir toward the *Compás del río*, not far from where Guada had been baptized, not far from where Shiro had thrown himself from the bridge and drifted away, but keeping clear from the zone where thieves and men of ill repute lived in muddy hovels.

'I shall not be leaving with you,' Shiro said. 'I have decided to stay for a time. Please convey my respects and apologies to the Lord and assure him of my fealty. Tell him my heart has been compromised and I must see to it. Tell my mother not to fret, to be patient, that I shall keep my promise to her.'

'I am saddened to hear this, Shiro-San,' Hasekura Tsunenaga replied, 'for the journey is long and treacherous, and your company shall be missed. Despite my warnings about what might happen to him if he returns to Sendai, the Friar will be aboard. Months more of him at close quarters . . . I do not know how I shall stand it.'

'Save the Shogun some firewood,' Shiro said, 'and toss him into the sea.'

'Perhaps I will,' said Hasekura Tsunenaga. 'What is more galling still is that six of the remaining Samurai from Edo, the ones who have taken their conversion too seriously, have chosen to remain here, as well, for fear of persecution back home. But not the priest!'

They approached the *Torre de Oro*, built by the Moors with mud and limestone in the early 13th century.

'I shall try and convince them otherwise, Hasekura-San, and if I am unable, I will help them get settled here.'

By the time Shiro and Guada travelled with the Delegation to Sanlúcar in order to see the ship off, most of the nobility in Sevilla had
turned against them. Their only allies, significant ones but sympa-
thetic to Guada only, were Don Rodrigo and Doña Soledad.

In the newborn grandson that Guada named Rodrigo, her father
had his heir. Neither the shameful demise of Julian, nor the manner
in which the child had been conceived, nor the scandalous nature of
his daughter's relationship with the foreigner mattered to him when
compared with the joy he felt at seeing his line continue.

And there were other considerations. He knew from the Duke of
Lerma that Shiro, for some reason, had become a favorite of the
King, and the King himself had told Rodrigo in what high esteem
he regarded Guada. Adding his own dose of slander to the rest, including that of his wife who blathered on about nothing else, would
only diminish his stature at court.

After the Delegation's ship sailed, they made the trip once again to
Medina-Sidonia and stayed for a time with Rosario. Returning to
the Duke's ancestral home, a place he thought he would never see
again, moved Shiro in a way he could not explain. They watched
the two baby boys play upon a large Alpujarreño coverlet spread
out in the garden where Guada and Shiro had first met. Rosario was
discrete and kind to them. The young women who had once been
so far apart in many respects found themselves sharing a great deal,
not only widowhood and motherhood, but public censure. An excursion was planned to Baelo Claudia for sentimental reasons, but
the young women decided the winds might have an untoward effect
upon the little boys. After *Semana Santa,* Shiro and Guada set out
for Sevilla again, this time by way of Ronda.

In that gentle mountain town and sporting the quiver and arrows given to him by the King, Shiro gave an exhibition one day for the *Hermandad del Santo Espíritu* of archery from horseback. The local nobles, more impressed with his skill than suspicious of his relation with the daughter of a Grandee of Spain, feted him.

That night, from a room that had a ceiling decorated with calligraphy quoting the Koran, that looked across to distant hills rising above the Río Guadiaro, they could see the occasional *cortijo* lit by firelight.

– XLVII –

In which Guada returns to La Moratalla

Two months later, Guada was pregnant again. Once certain of her state, she paid a visit to her aunt. She had not been back to the palacete since the day her father returned from Madrid with the news of Julian's detention. In light of what she had been through during the time she lived there, it felt like a second home, and despite her trepidation about how Doña Soledad might receive her news, it comforted her to walk its halls again.

Aunt and niece took the midday meal together in the same room where they had once discussed Guada's approaching marriage.

'I am with child,' Guada said.

Doña Soledad, dressed in black for the anniversary of the death of her oldest son, raised a spoon filled with chilled almond soup to her lips and savored it before replying.

'Congratulations, my dear. Are you pleased?'
  'Very,' said Guada.
  'Does anyone else know?' her aunt asked.
  'Only Shiro. I wanted to tell you first.'

THE SAMURAI OF SEVILLE

Soledad smiled, trying to hide her nerves. She closed her eyes for a moment and came to a decision.

'I am honored by your confidence, Guada. Might I give you some advice?'

'That is why I am here.'

'If you remain in Sevilla, it will be a nuisance for you with each passing month. Not only because of the society we live in, but because of your mother. I suggest that you and your gentleman friend move into La Moratalla. I shall come with you. But we will tell all of those concerned that we are travelling to Italy. It will be easier for you to present the new baby next year as a fait accompli.'

'La Moratalla . . .' said Guada, casting her gaze to the side.

'You disapprove of the idea?'

'No,' she said, looking back at her aunt. 'It is a wonderful idea, it is only that it was there that Julian and I went after our wedding.'

'It is my home,' Soledad said. 'Someday it will belong to you and your children. Better that you wash away any sad memories by putting new ones in their place. Does your friend know you were there with Julian?'

'No.'

'Then it shall be our secret. You will see that after only a short while, all your concerns will evaporate into the heavens.'

Don Rodrigo and Doña Inmaculada were alarmed and riled to lose sight of their grandson for such a long time. They vigorously tried to convince Guada to leave him in their care. But they were also relieved at the thought of their daughter's absence for a year under the wing of Soledad Medina, the most esteemed doyenne of their world.

The threesome and the child and a small contingent of servants set off for the estate in May. Guada began to show in June. Doña Soledad had not spent so much time there since she had been Guada's age, and what first seemed like a sacrifice soon became a great satisfaction. The gardens were preened and mulched into shape, the statues cleaned, leaks in the massive manse repaired. The servants particular to the house were drilled back to snuff or dismissed and replaced. The orange and lemon groves behind the house were neatened and raked, their slender trunks painted with whitewash.

Despite what she had heard from her niece and from the Duke, Doña Soledad maintained serious misgivings about the foreigner and his claim to be a Prince. But once they had settled in at La Moratalla, he won her over. His reserved manner, his love for her land, his demeanor and aristocratic bearing, his unashamed enthusiasm for flowers, his penchant for cleanliness, and, above all, the love he showered upon her niece coaxed her into their camp. His was not the Spanish version of masculinity she had known all her life. He exhibited no pretense of gruffness, no affected graveled voice. His good manners were not fraudulent or theatrical or mixed with questionable taste and a flair for vulgarity.

They occupied suites at extreme ends of the finca, and as the estate was equidistant from the two provincial capitals, Doña Soledad, when retiring to her rooms in the evening, would say, 'I'm off to Sevilla,' and Guada would reply, '*Vaya Usted con Dios*. We shall be on our way to Córdoba soon.' They never left the grounds or felt a need to. When the priest came on Sundays from the Real Monasterio de San Francisco in Palma del Río, Doña Soledad would attend mass in La Moratalla's chapel accompanied by her chambermaid.

Guada attended, as well, hidden by a *celosia* on the balcony built for a choir.

There was a Roman ruin on the property, two stone columns in the woods where they sometimes took picnics. During the oppressive summer months, they would go down by the Guadalquivir, which flowed along the estate's southern perimeter. The river was narrow there, but clear and deep, and Shiro would swim, carrying the little boy with him as the women watched and called out their worries from the shade.

Autumn arrived, cooling the evenings and cleansing the air. The days grew tender. The only other place Shiro had felt so at home was in Sendai, a place he tried to keep present in his thoughts even though, with each passing day, he felt more connected to the Andalusian arcadia surrounding him.

One night in late September toward the end of her eighth month, they lay awake in bed. Two candles flickered. They listened to owls and the fountains.

'Do you know what my aunt fears most?' she asked. 'That you will take me away from her before she dies. Far away to Japan.'

It was an eventuality Shiro thought about often. He wished to see his mother and to show his face once again to Date Masamune so that the Lord would continue to approve of him. He was still a Samurai, not a renegade Ronin.

'I must return at some point,' he said. 'But the journey is inhospitable and dangerous. It is not for a woman like you or for small children. I suffer about this whenever I think about it.'

It was the kind of conversation she had always hoped to have as a married woman, but it had never happened when she had been with Julian. She wished it would always be like this.

'I would like to know the land you come from,' she said. 'I would like to meet your mother and for our child to know where its father was born. Women 'like me' have sailed many times to the New World.'

'We can wait,' he said. 'I've no desire to sadden your aunt.'

'It may be for some time,' she said. 'She is still a vigorous woman.'

'That she is,' he said, laughing in the dark.

He kissed her shoulder.

Two weeks later she went into labor. The *comadrona* was awakened in the middle of the night and brought to their room by Doña Soledad's chambermaid. With difficulty, a baby girl was delivered just before dawn. Guada was badly torn and bled profusely. Shiro held her hand and stood by in silence as the color drained from her face. Doña Soledad sank to her knees and prayed.

– XLVIII –

In which Shiro makes a promise

Soledad Medina watched as he bathed her niece, kissed her good-bye, tied the shroud about her. They buried her next to the Roman ruin in the woods near a bluff overlooking the river where the baby was baptized a week later. Following Guada's wishes, the child was christened Soledad María.

Before returning to Sevilla, Shiro visited the gravesite to plant what was left of the Biwa seeds. In Japanese, he copied the poem his mother had left upon her first husband's grave, one he had memorized from his youth. He wrote it on a plain piece of paper and weighed it down upon the grass with a stone.

When snow falls my eyes sting
In winter I saw you
When the hashidoi blooms my breast rises
In spring I embraced you
When cicadas sing my limbs grow heavy
In summer I loved you
When leaves die my breath deserts me
In autumn you left me

Upon learning how his daughter had succumbed to a Florentine fever, Don Rodrigo began to weep. Doña Inmaculada fainted. The little boy was given to them. Doña Soledad decided to remain silent for a time about the little girl.

Shiro gathered his belongings and moved into the palacete with his baby daughter. A wet nurse came to the mansion and lived there for four months. Shiro encouraged the six Samurai who had stayed behind to settle in Coria del Río, where he had been so well attended. He gave them names and a letter of introduction and told them there was a good living to be had harvesting caviar from the sturgeon in the river there so close to the sea. Though he never went back to the village, the other Samurai prospered there and in time took Spanish wives.

After a year had passed, Doña Soledad sensed what was coming and unable to bear the silence any further called Shiro to her sitting room one morning after breakfast. Both of them still wore black.

'I wish to reiterate how welcome you are to live here until your dying day,' she said. 'You are young and may at some point wish to remarry, and were that to happen, I would still embrace your company.'

He bowed to her.

'I am leaving all of my possessions to the little one,' she said, 'all of my estates and income and savings. It will be for you to share in and to administer until she is grown into a young woman, something I doubt I shall live long enough to see.'

They both knew what she was doing, trying whatever she could to get him to stay.

'I must return to my country,' he said. 'And I must take my daughter with me. I cannot be sure how people here will react as she grows older. I hope you can forgive me.'

'Your daughter will one day be the envy of Sevilla,' she said, not giving in. 'She will be exquisitely beautiful and belong to its finest family. And if you will excuse the vulgarity, she will be extremely rich, as you too shall be. I know you have come to feel affection for this country, and you have powerful friends here. I beg of you to stay, or to leave her with me.'

He rose and walked to a window, looking down at the garden where a path lined with boxwood ended at a stone bench flanked by two palm trees. Birds were flittering about. He tried to imagine this woman when she was young and in love with the Duke, and the image softened him. He closed his eyes, then opened them and turned to her.

'We shall have to go,' he said. 'I have a solemn promise to keep. My honor demands it. But we could return afterwards.'

This was something, she thought. It was not a lot. And only God knew what might befall them on such an infernal journey, or how the young man might feel when reacquainted with his own. Life, she knew, had a way of branching forward. It rarely doubled back.

'Then perhaps you might make a solemn promise to me,' she said. 'Promise you will return her to me, so that she can see what she has here, what will be waiting for her, for as long as necessary. Promise me you will give her the chance to choose for herself.'

He saw no way out of it. Not only that, but his broken heart filled with gratitude. He came up to her, bowed, and then knelt before

257

her to kiss her fragile hand. 'I promise I shall bring her back to you,' he said.

'Then do not tarry, Shiro-San,' she said through her tears, 'for I shall not live forever, and if I die before seeing her again, mine will be the cruelest death ever recorded.'

'We shall return in four years' time,' he said, 'and remain long enough for her to reach an age of reason.' And he meant it, even though he had little idea how he might make it so.

'Take good care of her,' she said, grabbing on to him.
'I shall protect her with my life,' he said.

The ship sailed from Sanlúcar three months later, bound for Santa Cruz de Tenerife and La Habana. The Samurai stood on the forecastle holding little Soledad María in his arms. She was wrapped in a shawl that had been Guada's. Father and daughter looked back at the receding coast of Spain. Shiro recalled the first time he had seen it from the deck of the San José, unaware of what awaited him and how he had remained on board an extra night before setting foot on Spanish soil.

Despite the pain and misfortune that beset him there, it had entered his heart and changed him. When he arrived he was a callow lad still pretending to be a warrior. He was leaving it a man, a Samurai of his own making. Would they reach Japan safely? Would his Lord be cross with him? Would Sendai still feel like home? Would his mother still be alive? He remembered the last thing she said to him, 'Love your loneliness. Do not let it go. Treasure it with all your heart.' The word for lonliness in Spanish was *soledad*. With Guada gone, this was now his task.

The ship moved upon the sea. His little girl breathed easily. It was good to be alive.